"I have considered marrying ~~me.~~ Morton Pendergast," Victoria confessed.

"I've known him since I was a teenager. He's a few years older than me. Goes to our church. He has a very nice house, and a great job, and he thinks the world of Jonathan."

Buck's hand slipped over hers and he gave it a gentle squeeze. "But you don't love him, do you?"

Her eyes widened and she jerked her hand from his "Why would you say that?"

"A woman in love doesn't talk about her man like that. Sounds like you're only considering marriage as a way to secure a good life for you and your son. I get the impression there's no love for the man."

Her eyes flashed with fire. "That's a rotten thing to say. You make me sound like a—"

He broke in. "A woman who'd say yes out of need?"

"I'd never do that!" Victoria retorted defensively.

"Well, you just said you were considering marrying the man, but not once have you mentioned love."

They rode along in silence, Victoria's heart pounding with outrage.

"I think I could love him," she confessed finally. "In time."

"That's a lousy way to start a marriage, Tori, I think we both know that."

She had to change the subject. He was getting much too close to reality.

JOYCE LIVINGSTON is a real Kansas "lady" who lives in a little cabin that her husband built overlooking a lake. She is a proud grandmother who retired from television broadcasting, but she keeps very busy lecturing and teaching about quilting and sewing. She is also a part-time tour escort, which takes her to all kinds of fantastic places. She has had books and articles published on sewing, quilting, crafts, cooking, parenting, travel, personal color, and devotions—you name it. In 2000, she was voted **Heartsong**'s favorite new author. Joyce invites you to visit her website: joyce@joycelivingston.com. She adds, "I love hearing from my readers, and I answer every note, letter, and tear sheet.

HEARTSONG PRESENTS

Books by Joyce Livingston
HP353—Ice Castle
HP382—The Bride Wore Boots

Northern Exposure

Joyce Livingston

Heartsong Presents

I dedicate this book to Rebecca Germany, my Editor, for taking a chance on me as a new author.

And to Pauline Mitchell, my sister-in-law, who promotes my books to everyone with whom she comes in contact.

And to the **Heartsong** readers. Because of you, I was named Favorite New Author of the Year. Keep those letters and cards and survey sheets coming! I love hearing from you!

A note from the author:
I love to hear from my readers! You may correspond with me by writing: **Joyce Livingston**
Author Relations
PO Box 719
Uhrichsville, OH 44683

ISBN 1-58660-319-1

NORTHERN EXPOSURE

All Scripture quotations, unless otherwise noted, are taken from the King James Version.

All of the characters and events in this book are fictitious. Any resemblance to actual persons, living or dead, or to actual events is purely coincidental.

Cover design by Robyn Martins.

PRINTED IN THE U.S.A.

"Therefore I will look unto the LORD;
I will wait for the God of my salvation:
my God will hear me."
Micah 7:7

one

"Hi, Jason, it's me. I'm in Seward, Alaska, waiting for Mom. The cruise ship anchored about an hour ago. She should be getting off any minute. Any word from the bank?"

Victoria Whitmore leaned her head to one side and braced the phone against her shoulder, then shuffled her notebook under her arm, nearly dropping it when she heard her brother's answer. "They did? They approved our loan? Yippee! That means Mom and I are going to be able to open our gift shop after all. Everything hinged on that bank loan. I can hardly wait to tell her. How soon can we get the money?"

The smartly dressed young woman wearing a victorious smile listened intently to her lawyer brother. "Three weeks, huh? That's not bad, Jason. I was afraid it'd take much longer. Oh, this is exciting. Mom's gonna be so pleased." Victoria checked her watch. "We're really going to do it—open our own shop. I'm glad you and the boys agreed with me that Mom needs something challenging. She's gone through some pretty tough times since Dad died. I can't believe I got that stupid three-day flu and couldn't go with her on this cruise. I'm amazed she went alone."

Victoria glanced toward the double doors. "I'm not sure where we'll be in Alaska. Mom just said to pack a suitcase and meet her in Seward. If I get a chance, I'll call you again in a few days and let you know where we are. We should be home a week from today. Well, better go now. I want to greet Mom

5

with the good news when she gets off the ship. Bye, Jason, and thanks for everything. And say hi to Jonathan for me."

After hanging up the phone, Victoria moved to her seat, pulled her ballpoint pen from her purse, and flipped through her notebook. She checked and rechecked the figures for the new gift shop.

This week in Alaska will probably be the last vacation Mom and I will have for a very long time. Victoria entered a new idea in the notebook. *With the responsibility of opening a new shop, we're both going to be stuck in Kansas City. At least until we get it off the ground and into a paying proposition. I'm going to make every minute count while we're in Alaska.*

"This seat taken?"

Startled, Victoria looked up at a man clad in a western-cut leather jacket. She shifted her position and surveyed all the empty chairs in the room. Why did he have to pick one near her? Cautiously she answered, "No, it's not."

"Good." The stranger extended his hand and a warm smile. "I'm Buck."

Reluctantly she accepted his hand, flinching at his firm grasp. She watched out of the corner of her eye as the attractive, bearded man in faded jeans lowered himself into the nearby chrome and vinyl chair.

It was not her policy to carry on a conversation with a stranger, especially a male stranger. His unsolicited friendliness made Victoria uncomfortable, and she found herself pulling back into her shell, the shell she'd created for herself eight years ago. With a second glance about the room, she wondered why he'd selected that particular chair, when he probably had another hundred from which to choose. Hopefully, her mother would be coming through those doors soon and they'd be on their way.

What a hard time she'd had convincing her mother to go on the cruise alone! But the tickets were nonrefundable, and

Victoria and her mother had too much invested to let two tickets go unused. One unused ticket was bad enough. She was hoping the cruise line would relent and at least refund part of her money since she'd been too ill to take the trip. She just hoped Abigale had made a few friends and not stayed to herself. Good thing she'd taken her cross-stitch project, along with some books.

"Meeting someone coming in on the ship?" Buck asked, interrupting Victoria's thoughts.

"My mom."

He gave her a big grin as he stuffed his thumbs through his belt loops and settled his long frame into the uncomfortable chair. "Oh? Your mom, huh? I'm meeting my dad. He won this cruise in a drawing on the local radio station. I hated for him to come by himself, but he said he didn't mind. He's probably spent the week trying to avoid a shipboard romance. For an old geezer, he's good-looking and too smart to be taken. I reckon he's made it through unscathed."

Their eyes met. "You don't believe those things really happen, do you?" Victoria asked. "Shipboard romances? I think they only happen in fiction." She frowned. Surely situations like that only happened on television, never in real life. Not often anyway. She'd never heard of it actually happening to a real person. You would have to be pretty desperate to fall for a total stranger onboard a cruise ship.

"I don't know." A hearty laugh boomed from somewhere within his broad chest. "I've heard some pretty good stories. All those widows looking for rich old men. What better place to look than on a cruise ship?"

Victoria winced as he pulled a knife from a leather sheath on his belt and began carefully whittling on a frayed fingernail.

"Hey, my mother's a widow and she'd never do anything to encourage a shipboard romance," she responded defensively. She tucked an errant strand of hair behind her ear and turned her attention back to her notebook. She didn't want to talk, not after getting the good news from her brother. What she really wanted to do was think about the shop that would soon be a reality and plan how she would arrange the shelving, counters, and racks in the building they hoped to lease.

"Some women do strange things when they're lonely," Buck teased. He folded the knife and placed it back in the case. His eyes sparkled with mischief.

A frown creased Victoria's brow as she eyed him suspiciously, not sure exactly how to take his comment. "*Some* women? How about *some* men?"

He grinned, crossed his arms over his chest, and thrust his long legs into the narrow aisle. "Aw, come on now. Those cute little silver-haired ladies bat their sexy blues at a lonely guy, and bingo. Matrimony! Before the guy knows what hit him, the knot's tied and he's committed for the rest of his life. And so is his money!"

Victoria stiffened, her female feathers slightly ruffled, not sure if he was serious or just putting her on. "Maybe your father's the one who's on the prowl for a lonely, rich widow. Ever think of that?"

He crossed his ankles and spread his long arms across the adjoining chair backs. After a loud chuckle, he said, "Hey, I'm only kidding. My dad would never do that."

"You had me going there for a minute," she declared with relief, wishing this conversation had never started. "I know my mother would never be a party to a shipboard romance."

"Then I guess both our parents are safe. We can feel sorry for those who are more gullible." He smiled and winked. "I'm an old worrywart where my dad's concerned. Don't know why. He's taken good care of himself since my mom died six years ago. He's my best friend and sort of my business partner. I don't want any woman taking him away from me." Buck grinned. "We're getting along just fine the way things are. You know, the parent becomes the child and the child becomes the parent thing?" He made a gesture as if he were tipping his hat. "Sorry if I offended you. I didn't mean anything by my words, just making friendly conversation. Guess we Alaskans never see a stranger. We'll talk to anyone that'll listen." He glanced around the sparsely filled room. "I'm sure your mother behaved as a perfect lady on her cruise."

Victoria's brows lifted and she snickered aloud. "That's because she *is* a perfect lady. The last thing she'd want to do is seduce your father and move to Alaska."

"Hey, Alaska's not such a bad place to live. Ask any Alaskan."

"Well, that may be true. But my mom and I have plans."

She watched as a uniformed security guard moved toward the double doors. Surely the passengers would be unloading soon. How long could it take to get through customs?

"Plans?" he asked, apparently interested in her comment.

She closed her notebook. Deciding he looked harmless enough, she answered, "When we get back to Missouri after this vacation, we're going to open a gift shop together. It's been our lifelong dream. I'm an artist, and I plan to sell a lot of my work there." She smiled triumphantly, her good news still fresh on her mind, and closed the notebook in her lap.

"Artist, huh? I'll bet you're a good one. You don't paint any of those funny things that look like the guy poured paint on canvas and then stepped in it barefooted, do you?"

She had to laugh at his description of abstract art. "No, I'm more the Thomas Kinkade type of artist. You know, landscapes, trees, flowers, country settings. But what I enjoy the most is portraits."

"Well, I do want to apologize—about the way I talked about your mother. I'm sure she's a very nice person."

"Your apology isn't necessary. I understand about your dad. I do the same thing with my mom. Protect her, that is. She's my best friend, too. We're fortunate to still have our parents. Many of my friends have lost their parents." Victoria pushed back the sleeve of her jacket and checked her watch. "Shouldn't they be coming soon?"

The words had barely passed her lips when the security guard opened one of the double doors. Disembarking passengers began elbowing through the narrow opening, pushing overflowing carts laden with bulging suitcases.

"Mom!" Victoria jumped to her feet and waved her arms wildly. "Over here!"

A tall slender woman clad in a coral pantsuit smiled and waved back. "Victoria, hi. You made it! I wasn't sure you would."

"There's my dad. Been nice visiting with you," Buck volunteered and nodded. He pushed past Abigale Whitmore and her daughter. "Dad! Dad! Over here."

The two women embraced.

"Mom! I just talked to Jason, he heard from the bank. We got the loan. Aren't you excited?"

Abigale threw her arms about her daughter and squeezed her tight. "Oh, Honey, this is such good news for you—"

"For us, Mom, for us. We're going to be partners. It's *our* gift shop." Victoria clasped her mother's hands in hers and stepped back for a better look at the woman. "You must've had a good trip, you're positively glowing. I'm so sorry I had to cancel at the last minute. I really wanted to go on that cruise with you. But it looks like you had a good time without me."

"I did, Victoria. I had a wonderful time. I can hardly wait to tell you all about it," Abigale exclaimed, her green eyes bright and shining. "The most amazing things happened!"

It was good to see her mother excited like this. Even with silver hair, no one would guess Abigale was sixty-two. Victoria smiled to herself, remembering Buck's comment about silver-haired women. The past year had been a difficult one for Abigale. Losing the husband she'd married as a teenager had taken its toll. She'd withdrawn from nearly everyone, even her best friends. Victoria and her brothers had worried about their mother. They were surprised when she agreed to go on the

Alaskan cruise, the same cruise she and Guy Whitmore had planned to take on their forty-fifth wedding anniversary.

"And I want to hear every little detail. I hope you took lots of pictures," Victoria rattled on, unable to contain her enthusiasm. "The family has planned a welcome home party for us when we get back, so we'd better get your film developed before we head to Kansas City." She paused thoughtfully. "By the way, where are we going from here? Your message just said to pack for a week in Alaska and meet you here in Seward. Are we going on a tour bus? Or the domed excursion train?" Victoria glanced around at the crowd pressing in around them. "You didn't leave much information on my answering machine when you called from the ship."

"Not at fifteen dollars a minute, I didn't. That's the cost of a ship-to-shore phone call. You're the one who offered to meet me at the end of the cruise so we could have some time together after you had to cancel. Remember? And besides, I need to—"

"Sure I remember, and I meant it. I might have missed the cruise, but I'm well now and ready to see Alaska, if you're not too tired after a week on the ship." The young woman took stock of the area with a concerned look. "Mother, where's your luggage?"

"Dear, that's one of the things I want to tell you—"

Victoria frowned as her palm moved swiftly to her cheek. "Oh, no. They didn't lose your luggage, did they? Oh, Mom, surely not."

A man's deep voice boomed from behind them, "Dad, where are you going? I'm parked in the other direction."

The two women turned to find Buck following a tall, slender man who Victoria decided was Buck's father.

"Oh, I see you found your dad," she acknowledged, noting he seemed rather perturbed by something.

He nodded his head toward the man. "Oh, hello again. Yes, I found him."

The older man abruptly stopped the cart beside the two women.

Victoria smiled, feeling rather awkward, not knowing if she should try to introduce them to her mother or just turn away. "I found her, but not her luggage. I guess it didn't—"

"It's right here. I have it on my cart," Buck's father declared proudly. He motioned toward the floral tapestry suitcases standing alongside his. "See? All safe and sound."

Buck stopped in his tracks with a puzzled look on his face. "You have her luggage on your cart? Maybe I'd better try to run down another cart, Dad. I'm parked in the lot on the east side of the building. The ladies may not be going that direction."

"I'll get a cart for her, you needn't bother," Victoria volunteered quickly. She gestured toward an empty chair. "Just put her luggage there so she can sit down while I go after the cart. That way you two won't be delayed. And thank you for bringing it for her," she added with a nod. "I'm glad she didn't have to juggle it herself."

"No, I'll get it. You three stay here. It'll only take me a minute." Buck slid his hand under his father's elbow and motioned him toward a chair. "Sit down, Dad."

Ron Silverbow pulled free of his son's grasp. He stood straight and tall. "No need, Son. I'll handle Abigale's luggage myself. Right, Abbey?"

"Right, Ron," Abigale agreed. Smiling, she moved to stand beside the older man and slipped her hand into the crook of his arm.

Buck shot a quick look at Victoria as if to say, *Do you have any idea what is going on here? Because I sure don't.*

She returned the look with a shrug of her shoulders.

The older man, quite handsome with his silver-gray hair and straight, chiseled features, gestured toward the questioning young woman. "You must be Abigale's daughter, Victoria. You're just as pretty as your mother described you. And you're almost as pretty as your mom. You've already met Buck. Right?"

Both Victoria and Buck nodded and glared at one another in stunned silence.

"Well, Abigale," Ron said as he wrapped his fingers over hers and patted them gently. "You haven't met him. This is my son, Buck. He's a good kid, but he tries to keep me on a short rope sometimes. He has a tendency to forget I'm the senior here."

Abigale snickered and reached toward the younger man. "Nice to meet you, Buck. I've heard so much about you and Micah. I've looked forward to meeting both of you."

Victoria quickly moved to her mother's side. "Who's Micah?"

"My son," Buck answered bluntly; his glare fixed on his father.

"Did you bring the minivan like I told you, Son?"

Buck nodded. "Just like you said on the telephone. But I still don't understand why it had to be the minivan. You didn't buy that many Alaskan souvenirs, did you?"

"Not hardly. I *live* in Alaska, remember? As a matter of fact, I didn't buy any souvenirs at all. Not a one," Ron admitted. He chuckled, then winked at the lovely gray-haired woman standing beside him. "But I *am* bringing something special home with me."

"Then why the minivan, Dad? Why not my pickup?"

Ron Silverbow looked first to Buck, then to Victoria, and then to Abigale. "Why don't we sit down while the crowd thins out and the parking lot empties a bit?"

"But—" Buck started.

"Just sit, Buck. We're in no hurry."

The three took seats while Ron stood before them, tall and proud.

"I'm sure you two kids have figured out by now that Abigale and I met on the ship. First night, actually. I was sitting at a table on the open deck, wishing your mama had lived long enough to take this cruise with me, and feeling sorry for myself, I might add, when the music started to play and the cruise director announced a line dance."

He paused and stepped aside to allow a pregnant woman and her cart to pass.

"Well," Ron continued, "he instructed his staff of attractive young ladies and gents to fetch themselves partners from the audience. When one of them approached me, I backed off, but she wouldn't take no for an answer and pulled me onto the deck."

"Same thing happened to me," Abigale interjected excitedly, never taking her eyes off Ron's weathered face. "A young man in a blue blazer and white slacks took my hand and pulled me onto the deck with the other dancers. At first, I was mortified. Then, I thought, I'm on a cruise, and this is what they do on cruises. And I actually learned to line dance."

The young woman cupped her hand over her mother's sleeve. "Mother, you didn't! You and Daddy never danced. You never wanted to."

"Oh, but I did," her mother confessed. "Your father was the one who never wanted to."

"It was fun, wasn't it, Abigale?" Ron asked, his handlebar mustache tilting upward as he spoke. "Even though I was all feet till you came to my rescue."

Victoria watched in horror as she caught her mother's new friend winking at her mother a second time.

Abigale grinned. "You were very graceful, once you caught on. I was proud of you."

"So, if you were each dancing with a staff member, how did you get together?" Victoria asked. She found it nearly impossible to believe her timid mother would actually do the line dance, or any dance, with a stranger.

"Well, when the first number ended, I was going to leave the dance area, but my partner swung me around and said she was going to get another partner and for me to dance with the lady next to me, who happened to be Abigale. I'll tell you, I was embarrassed. So was she. But that instructor took Abbey's hand and placed it in mine. What could we do? Right, Kid?"

"Right, Ronnie." Abigale blushed.

Kid? Victoria thought. *He called my sixty-two-year-old mother kid?*

"Dad!" Buck chastised as he quickly rose to his feet.

"Let me finish, Son." Ron clasped his hand firmly over Buck's arm. "That happened the first night. Me and Abbey danced that line dance thing till most of the others dropped out, then we went into the lounge and talked about our families till it got dark." He gave a good belly laugh. "And in Ketchikan, Alaska, this time of year it's about one in the morning before it gets dark. And since the sun was coming up in a couple of hours, we stayed up for the sunrise too."

"So, didn't you meet anyone else onboard?" Victoria asked. As soon as the words came out of her mouth, she wished she hadn't asked.

"Sure, Honey, lots of nice people. You'd be surprised how many people our age take cruises. And they have so many activities you could be busy every waking hour. I'm so sorry you got the flu and couldn't go at the last minute. But if you'd gone, I might not have met Ron."

That was a fine thing to say, Victoria thought, surprised at her mother's candor. *Sounds like she didn't even miss me.*

"And I'm sure glad that didn't happen," Ron said. "Your mother and I had a great time. Spent every minute of every day together. And like I said, in Alaska. . .the days last into the night."

"Way into the night," Abigale added with a raise of her brow. "Ron took good care of me, Victoria. Your fears about me going on the cruise alone were foolish. I was perfectly safe, and rarely alone."

"So it seems," Victoria muttered. *Safe and rarely alone? Oh, dear. What has she gotten herself into? She's not old enough to be senile.*

Buck checked his watch nervously. "This is interesting, hearing how you two met, but shouldn't we be going, Dad, and let the ladies be on their way? I'm sure they have plans. And we've got a long way to go."

"No hurry, Son. Park it." Ron pointed to the chair formerly occupied by Buck. "The story gets more interesting as it goes along. And I'm not finished yet."

Victoria shot a questioning glance at her mother who seemed to have no concern about where they were going from here.

"Like I said, we spent every minute together. I've lived in Alaska all my life, but seeing it through Abigale's eyes was like seeing it for the first time. Her enthusiasm for its beauty opened my eyes to things I'd never seen or appreciated."

He stepped forward and placed his hand on Abigale's shoulder. "And we talked for hours and hours."

He turned and let out a slight chuckle. "Why, Victoria, I know you and your brothers so well I could probably tell you things even your closest friends don't know about you."

He returned his gaze to his son. "And Abbey knows everything about my family. We swam together in both the indoor and outdoor pools, sunned on the decks, played bingo, shuffleboard, and even batted a few tennis balls. We ate at the midnight buffet every night, we rode the tram up Mount Roberts in Juno. We did it all together. We even prayed together. She loves our Lord as much as I do."

Abigale gave him a smile of approval. "I sure do."

Ron Silverbow removed his hand from Abigale's shoulder and extended his open palm as a smile lit up her face. She placed her hand in his and rose to stand by his side. He slid his arm around her waist and pulled her close. "And together we've decided to stay. Victoria, Buck, Abigale and I are getting married!"

two

"You're what?" Buck hollered loud enough that the passersby stopped and turned to see where the commotion was coming from.

"Married? You and my mother?" Stunned and confused, Victoria instinctively reached for her mother's hand and pulled her away from the man who had just made his ridiculous announcement.

A uniformed officer left his post by the door and hurried over. "Anything wrong here, folks?"

Ron shook his head and smiled pleasantly. "Everything's fine, Officer. Just having a few family words. Sorry if we got a little carried away. We'll try to knock it down a few decibels."

The man looked from face to face, then moved away slowly with a backward glance over his shoulder. The passersby moved on, their attention once again turned to finding the right bus.

Victoria wanted to say something, anything, but the words refused to come. Surely, she'd misunderstood. "Oh, Mom," she stammered, "wh—what about the plans to open our shop?"

Abigale took her daughter's hand and squeezed it affectionately. "We'll talk about that later. Just the two of us. Okay, Dear?"

Victoria nodded, temporarily appeased.

"Dad?" Buck questioned in a hushed but firm voice. "Do you know what you just said?"

"I said exactly what I intended to say, Son. Abigale and I are getting married. Right, Sweetheart?" He gently tugged

17

Abigale away from Victoria's grasp. "I don't think our kids believe us."

Abigale smiled and stood by Ron. "Then we'll just have to convince them, Ronnie." She leaned into his side and beamed into his face. "Give them a little time. After all, I'm sure this is the last thing they expected to hear when they met us here."

"Mother!" Victoria blurted out, surprised to find her voice in working order once again. "This has to be a joke! And I'm not laughing. This isn't funny."

"Yeah, it's a joke, right?" Buck moved in. The frown eased from his face and he let loose a relieved chuckle. "You two had us going there for a minute. Married? That's pretty funny. Good joke."

Ron leaned over and planted a kiss on Abigale's forehead. "No joke. Is it, Honey?"

Abigale blushed as she turned toward her daughter. "I'm sorry, Victoria. I wish there was some way I could have warned you, given you a chance to get to know Ron and what a wonderful man he is before I told you we were planning on getting married. But we talked it over, and the best way seemed to be to tell you right up front."

Frustrated, Victoria threw her arms in the air. "But, Mom!"

"Dad!" Buck interrupted before Victoria could continue. "You're crazy! You can't meet a lady on a cruise ship, know her for seven days, and marry her!"

Ron wrapped his arms protectively around Abigale. "Oh, but I did. And I am! I love this woman, and we're going to spend the rest of our lives together. Aren't we, Sugar?"

"And where, may I ask, are you going to live?" Victoria questioned, wondering if they'd even considered that currently they lived eons apart. "In Alaska, Mother? Or are you planning to bring him to Missouri?"

"Dad could never survive a year in Missouri!" Buck reasoned aloud with a white-knuckled grasp on the luggage cart.

"And Mother couldn't take the Alaska cold," Victoria added

convincingly, allying herself with a stranger.

"Why don't you two let us decide that for ourselves. After all, we're quite capable of making our own decisions." Ron turned his attention to his son. "Buck, stack Victoria's luggage on top of ours, and we'll all head to the minivan."

"Mother! Where are we going? What about our trip?" Victoria stood with her hands on her hips. "What about our gift shop? Our dream?" She needed answers.

"We're going with Ron," Abigale replied softly, as if to cushion the blow they'd just dealt their children. "We're going to spend the next week at his place, the place I'll be living once we're married. We want the four of us to get to know one another."

"But, Dad!" Buck said with exasperation.

"Mom, you can't!" Victoria argued.

The pleas went unheeded by the newly engaged couple. The parents were already walking arm in arm toward the exit doors, leaving their children to bring the cart.

Victoria shot Buck a questioning look and accused through clenched teeth, "You knew about this, didn't you? You knew your dad was going to find himself a wife on that ship! You knew it all the time, and you didn't stop him!"

Buck gave her a frown. "Your mom went on that cruise alone. What does that tell you? She had her sights out for a good man and she found one. My vulnerable old father! I hope you're satisfied. Or were you a part of the plot?" He grabbed her suitcases and flung them on top of the others, then motioned to her. "Come on. Looks like their plans are all made. Guess we'll have to go along with them. For now!"

Victoria adjusted the strap on her shoulder bag and followed the big man toward the parking lot. "For now is right. We've got to talk them out of this!"

❧

"You drive," Ron ordered Buck when the last piece of luggage had been loaded into the minivan. "Victoria can sit up front with you, it'll give you two a chance to get acquainted. My honey and I will sit in the back."

Victoria watched as Ron ushered Abigale into the seat, then climbed in after her as she slid across. *He might as well have pulled her onto his lap, he is sitting so close*, Victoria thought.

Buck stood impatiently while Victoria climbed into the front seat, and then he closed her door with a slam. He went around and sat in the driver's seat. "Since I'm driving, don't you think it'd be nice if you'd tell me where I'm supposed to drive?" he asked sarcastically.

Ron leaned forward and placed his hand on the seat back behind his son. "First, let's find us a nice little restaurant and get us something to eat. My little sweetie and I are famished, and I'll bet you two kids are too. Right, Victoria?"

"Um, I guess so," Victoria muttered. She felt as out of control as a baby bird who'd just fallen out of its nest. "At this point, whatever the rest of you want to do is fine with me." She lifted her arms in defeat.

Ron continued. "After lunch, we'll take the beautiful drive up the coast to Anchorage. We'll be home by five or six tonight. That'll give us plenty of time to have an early dinner, and you ladies can get a good night's sleep."

Buck shoved the gearshift to neutral and turned to face his father, who was already deeply engrossed in conversation with Abigale. "All four of us?"

Ron stopped pointing and seemed surprised at his son's question. "Of course, all four of us. I already told you that. We're taking the ladies with us to Anchorage."

"But, Dad—"

Ron gave his son a pleasant but I-don't-want-to-hear-any-more-about-this grin. "Just do it, Son."

The minivan leaped forward as Buck shoved the gearshift into drive, pinning the foursome to their seats. Victoria was sure she heard Buck mumble something under his breath.

"Your dad always like this?" she asked softly, not wanting to interrupt the conversation in the backseat.

He sent a quick glance her way. "No. Sometimes he's worse."

"Parents. You think you know them, then they pull something like this." Victoria shrugged.

Buck pulled around a slow-moving car. "Tell me about it. I sure never expected this from my dad. He's always been so levelheaded."

"My mom too. She didn't even want me taking modern dance in gym class. Now she's line dancing with a total stranger from another country."

"Alaska isn't another country, Victoria."

"I know that! What I mean is—a place so far from home."

He gave a snort. "That stranger happens to be the father I thought I knew. Mr. Straight-laced himself. I don't even know that man sitting in the backseat making out with your mother."

Victoria crossed her arms indignantly. "I warned you, your father may have been playing Casanova with the ladies on the ship, but you wouldn't beli—"

"My father? How about your mother? The baby blue eyes? Remember? I'll bet your mom made the first move. My dad sure wouldn't!"

"Oh, he wouldn't? Well, he's doing a pretty good job of it right now! Just listen to him sweet-talking her in the backseat."

"Hey?" Ron asked as he leaned over the seat and lightly tapped Victoria's arm. "You two getting acquainted? You're gonna be related soon, you know."

"Yes, Victoria," Abigale volunteered as she leaned up beside Ron. "I do want the two of you to get along. Soon you'll be brother and sister. Isn't that sweet?"

The young woman in the front seat did a quick double take. "Brother and sister? Just what I need, another brother."

"Sure," Ron confirmed quickly. "Well, stepbrother and

stepsister. But that doesn't make any difference. We'll be one big happy family. I can hardly wait to meet the rest of your clan."

He reached forward and slapped his son on the shoulder. "Just think, Buck. You're gonna have five brothers."

Buck groaned. "That'll be fun," he replied coolly. "If there was anything I ever wanted, it was five brothers." He nodded toward Victoria. "And a sister."

"Well, you got them now!" Rod added proudly. "Soon as Abigale and Victoria have a good rest at our place, I'm gonna fly back to Kansas City with them to meet the boys. Want to come along, Son?"

Buck turned his shoulders toward his father but kept his eyes on the road. "I'd just love to make a trip to Missouri to meet my new kinfolk, Dad; but in case you have forgotten, I have a practice to run. I don't think my patients would appreciate it if their doctor didn't show up at the office for their appointments."

Victoria brightened. "You're a doctor? I thought you and your father were partners—in some sort of business venture."

Ron leaned over the seat again. "We are. We jointly own The Golden Nugget Lodge in Anchorage. His sainted mama left her half to Buck when she died."

"Oh," Victoria said, feeling the man's grief betrayed in his voice. "I'm sorry. About your wife, I mean."

"It's okay, Victoria. I'm sure everyone was wondering if I was gonna grieve myself to death. It's been a long time." He flung an arm around Abigale and hugged her close. "But I'm not grieving anymore. Not now that I have my Abbey to love."

Victoria cringed.

"Buck had just started his practice when his mama left us," he continued with a quick kiss to Abigale's forehead. "He helps me out when I need him. And he gives me financial advice. He's much better at figures than I am."

Ron reached across Abigale quickly and pointed toward

the deep green foothills that rose majestically at the edge of the road. "See them, Sweetie? A couple of Dall sheep clinging to the side of that cliff. Up there! See?"

The two women leaned toward the windows.

"Sure they aren't mountain goats, Dad?" Buck chided, apparently relieved at the change of subject as he maneuvered the minivan around a sharp curve.

"Hey, Son. This old guy knows a sheep from a goat. Next, you'll be telling me that eagle over there is a raven," Ron returned good-naturedly.

"Whoops, you're right," his son admitted as he took his eyes off the road long enough to sneak a peek at the two sheep moving slowly across the cliff's surface. "I should know better than to question you when it comes to Alaska's wild animals."

He turned to Victoria. "My dad has been hunting since long before I was born. He makes a great guide. Guess now that he's going to get married, his guiding days are over."

"You really think they'll go through with it?" Victoria whispered with her hand to her mouth. "Get married?"

Buck's face became serious, and Victoria could see the little vein in his temple ticking nervously. "I don't know, Victoria. I've never seen him like this. I don't know what to think. I only know—if they are serious—there are going to be plenty of adjustments in all our lives. We may be in for a bumpy ride."

Victoria thought about what he said as she gazed at the beauty of the bay. The blue water sparkled like a million dewdrops after an unexpected spring shower. The afternoon sun shone brightly in the cloudless sky. The lush green mountains rose out of the sea as if reaching to God Himself, each peak commanding attention with its pristine white frosting. The scene was more than Victoria had imagined it would be, better than the pictures in the travel brochures. *Purple mountain majesties.* She beheld their beauty as they rode along the highway. *No wonder the writer had coined such a phrase. Majestic is the perfect word to describe them.*

"I never tire of seeing them." Buck's words broke into her thoughts. "Alaskan mountains are like no others in the world."

"I can see why. They're beautiful," she conceded.

"Bet Missouri doesn't have anything like this." He smiled and raised a bushy brow.

"No, but I love Missouri. Is Anchorage pretty?"

"Sure is," he answered with pride. "We don't have the coastal beauty of some of the cities like Ketchikan and Juneau, but we have the snowcapped mountains nearby. All of Alaska is beautiful country."

"You ski?" she asked, truly interested in the country in which her mother claimed she was going to live.

"Sure. You?"

She screwed up her face. "Some. I'm not very good at it. We usually only get to Colorado a couple days each year. But I enjoy it. So does my son."

He frowned and turned his head slightly toward her. "You have a son?"

"Sure do. Jonathan. He's seven. He's staying at home with my brother and his wife while I'm on this vacation with Mom. I work for my brother as a research assistant, so Jonathan is used to being around his uncle. I miss Jonathan, but I'm sure he'll be fine. They love spoiling him. Probably enjoying his break from his doting, overly protective mother." She rolled her eyes.

"Micah's a little older than Jonathan." Buck shook his head ruefully. "If things go the way our parents plan, I guess those boys will be step-cousins."

"What you two talking about up there in the front seat?" Ron asked, his arm still wrapped around Abigale.

"Just getting acquainted, Dad."

A big smile curved across the elder man's face. "Good. Abigale and I want our kids to be friends. Carry on." He gave a mock salute and turned to his seatmate.

"Guess that means you're married, if you have a son. Your husband didn't come on this vacation with you?"

Victoria blinked her eyes and swallowed hard. Why did everyone always assume she had a husband? She did not have a husband, and she did not want to talk about it with this man, or anyone. "We live alone. The two of us."

He paused. "Sorry."

"For what? That I don't have a husband? Or that we live alone? We do just fine, thank you." She regretted the intonation in her voice.

He raised his brows and backed away from her and toward his door. "Wow. Sorry! Didn't mean to wake up sleeping dogs. Guess I touched a nerve."

She forced a slight smile. "You didn't. Wake up the dogs, I mean. It's just that—well, I'll explain it sometime. If—we become kinfolk, as your dad says."

"Well—if it's any consolation, my son and I live alone too. Guess you'll find out sooner or later, so I'll tell you myself. My wife and my mother were killed in a car-train accident six years ago. I should have died with them."

His words cut through any false pride of self-defense she had built up.

"I'm so sorry," she said sincerely. Her fingertips lightly touched his hand. "But why would you say such a thing? That you should have died with them? You have a son to raise. Surely you wouldn't want him to be without both parents, would you?"

"No." His answer was barely audible. "Of course not."

"You mustn't say such things. Life is too precious to wish for death." She was fumbling for words and she knew it. But what could you say to a man who had just told you the deepest hurt he'd ever had in his life? A hurt most people would never experience. Somehow, her predicament paled in light of his comments.

He straightened. "Oh, I didn't mean I wish I'd died with

them. I'm thankful I didn't. For Micah's sake. I meant I should have been in the accident with them. I was supposed to drive them to Nenana that day; but I had a patient about to deliver her baby, so my wife drove the car instead." His eyes clouded and he blinked several times before going on. "Maybe if I'd been at the wheel, maybe if—"

"You can't do that to yourself, Buck. Blame yourself like that. God—"

He turned to her sharply. "God? God what? God wanted to add angels to His heaven? My wife and mother had fulfilled their purposes on earth? I've heard all those flowery explanations, and they're all a bunch of bunk."

"Now, Buck," Ron warned as he caught the anguish in his son's voice. "You know you can't blame God for what happened to your mama and Claudette."

"Yeah? Then who shall I blame, Dad? If not God, who? He could have prevented that accident. He could have made that train cross the intersection one minute later. He could have caused a flat tire or mechanical breakdown so they wouldn't have been there at that exact moment. If God shouldn't be blamed, I guess there is only one person who should be blamed—me!" Buck's voice had risen to such a level it filled the minivan and frightened the occupants.

No one answered. There seemed to be nothing to say. The group rode along in silence. Soon Abigale's head was bobbing and Ron pulled her over onto his shoulder. Then he leaned his forehead against the window glass and stared outside. No doubt he was remembering the accident and the horrible loss of his wife and daughter-in-law.

After what seemed to be hours, Victoria gently placed her hand over Buck's. He turned his head slightly and in his eyes she could see the open wound still lingering after six long years. "I'm sorry, Buck. I know it doesn't help, but in some ways I understand what you're going through. My son was born with a twisted foot."

He took his eyes off the road. "I'm sure he's had surgery to correct it. Is he doing better now?"

She nodded. "I guess you could say that. He's been through so much, but it's been worth it. He limps, but his foot is nearly normal. He gets along fine."

"Guess he's got some more surgeries coming up in his future."

"Yes. Several."

"Hey, look. I'm a doctor and although I'm not an orthopedist, I'd like to hear more about his condition and take a look at that leg." He smiled. "When—and if—he becomes my nephew."

A feeble smile met his. "Sure. When—and if."

She shifted nervously in her seat, weighing her words before she spoke, wanting to say just enough and no more. "The rest of my story is different from yours too, and although I love God and He is Lord of my life—"

She lowered her head and added in a near whisper, "I'm as angry at God as you are. For several reasons."

With a raised brow, Buck did a quick double take.

She quickly looked into the backseat, making sure her mother was sleeping and Ron wasn't paying attention. She hadn't shared her feelings on this matter with her closest friends. "Oh, I live life on the outside like a good little Christian girl, but on the inside I'm filled with anger too. I've never told this to anyone, and I don't know why I'm telling you. I guess it's because I think you'd understand, going through all you have. I just wanted you to know that, and I hope we can become friends. Especially since we're apparently going to become relatives."

Buck slid his hand from beneath hers and placed it on top, then gave a little squeeze. "I'm ready to listen, whenever you want to talk about it."

three

Ron Silverbow twisted a lock of Abigale's silver hair around his finger as she lay sleeping in the backseat, her head leaning against his broad shoulder. *Abigale*. He repeated her name in his heart as he watched the even rise and fall of her breathing. *She is so beautiful. How could I be this lucky?*

He glanced at his son and Abigale's daughter. He hoped the two of them would get along. And he hoped they could understand the love he and Abigale felt for one another. He smiled to himself. *Love at my age? No wonder these kids were skeptical when Abigale and I told them we planned to get married.*

Abigale stirred slightly as she nestled closer to Ron. He grazed her hair lightly with his chin. *Well, no matter what the kids say, we're going to get married. Time is passing, and we don't intend to miss a minute of it.* He and Abbey had decided that before they had gotten off the ship. Since the first minute he had seen this woman, he knew she was something special; but little had he dreamed she would pay him any attention. She was soft and gentle. He was rugged and tough from years of guiding hunting trips through the wilderness. She was cautious and slow to speak. He was bold and ready to speak his mind, even if it went against other folk's grain. They were like opposites on the color wheel; but from his viewpoint, they complemented one another. *Yes*, he told himself with a grin of satisfaction, *Abbey and I belong together. And together we're going to be, no matter what our kids say.*

❧

"Dad?"

Ron stiffened. "What? You say something, Buck?"

Buck laughed as his eyes caught his father's in the rearview mirror. Even though his father was handsome for his age, the thought of the crusty old man sweeping a lovely, sophisticated woman off her feet on a cruise was ludicrous. Buck hoped he would be able to talk some sense into his father's head when they could be alone. "I was just telling Victoria how beautiful Alaska is up around Anchorage."

Victoria twisted in the seat so she could look at Ron. "I've heard it gets really cold in the winter. Did you tell my mom that?"

Ron nodded. "Now, Victoria, don't worry your pretty little head about that. We keep the Golden Nugget Lodge as warm as a sauna in the wintertime. Your mama won't even have to wear her longies unless she goes outside."

"Longies?" Buck repeated as he peered into the mirror. "She'd better wear her longies or the woman will freeze to death. If you're planning on keeping that woman in Alaska, the least you can do is be honest with her and get her some long underwear."

Victoria's eyes widened. "Really, Buck? It gets that cold?"

"Cold enough to freeze spit in midair."

"Buck!" Ron gave his son a shake of his finger. "Mind your manners. You're talking to a lady."

"Just being honest, Dad."

"Mom gets goose bumps when the temperature drops to thirty degrees in Kansas City."

Buck grinned to himself. *Thirty degrees? Wait until she sees how low the temperature can drop on the thermometer by the lodge's front door.*

"You two just never mind. I'll make sure my little butter-cup doesn't get too cold," Ron said.

"Mr. Silverbow, I—" Victoria began.

"Ron. Call me Ron."

"Ron," she began again. "Are you sure this isn't infatuation? I mean—seven days on a ship—"

Ron leaned forward, his quick movements waking Abigale. "Now listen to me, both of you. We're old enough to know the difference between love and infatuation. We've both been there, done that. We both loved our deceased spouses. That love will never change, and we'll never forget them. But—"

"But, Dad. Mom and—"

"Son! Will you put a sock in that mouth of yours and listen to your father for once in your life?"

Abigale rubbed at her eyes and stretched her arms. "What? What's going on? Have I been asleep long?"

"Not long, Sweetie." Ron patted her shoulder, then turned his attention back to the couple in the front seat. "I was just telling these two kids of ours how much we love each other. If they're as smart as I hope they are, they'll both shut up and be happy for us."

Buck shot Victoria a look of defeat.

"Of course they'll be happy for us," Abigale sweetly assured the silver-haired man whose arm cradled her shoulders. "Won't you, children?"

Good thing she slept through our discussion, Buck mused as he eyed the young woman in the seat beside him. She appeared to have decided to abandon her argument rather than upset her mother. Perhaps he'd better do the same. He cast a look in the mirror and caught his father staring at him, as if waiting for his response to Abigale's request.

"Victoria?" Abigale questioned.

"Ah—sure. I'm happy for you, Mom. At least I will be if you're happy."

"Buck?" Ron asked.

Buck gulped hard. He hated to agree, but he didn't want to upset either his father or Abigale any further. Besides, his argument didn't seem to have any weight with either of them. "Sure, Dad. Like Victoria said, if the two of you are happy, I'll be happy."

Victoria gave him a look that seemed to be saying, *Liar.*

And Buck felt like one.

&

The two in the front seat rode along silently while the couple in the backseat chattered on endlessly about their cruise and their plans for their future.

Oh, boy. Now what? Victoria wondered as she looked out the window. *Does this mean an end to the plans for our gift shop?*

"What?" Buck asked.

Victoria turned her head quickly. "Did you say something?"

Buck relaxed his hold on the steering wheel and grinned. "Not really. Just curious. Your eyes may have been looking at our beautiful scenery, but I get the feeling you weren't really seeing it. Am I right?"

The confused young woman sighed. She rotated her fingertips on her temples. "Guess I'm hurt. No, I'm mad! How could Mom do this to me? We've been planning to open this shop for over a year. Surely she doesn't think I'll go on and do this by myself. I could never manage it on my own."

"Look," Buck said quietly. "Don't give up yet. I don't know much about the shop you keep talking about, but if you and I work together, maybe we can convince our ditsy parents—"

"Ditsy!" she broke in.

His eyes darted to the rearview mirror, which reflected the pair in the backseat. They were caught up in their own conversation and paying no attention to their children. "Yeah, ditsy. I think that pretty well describes them, don't you?" Buck smiled.

Victoria thought it over and decided he was right. Ditsy was a good name for the way their parents were behaving. "Ditsy."

They snickered like two kids sharing a secret.

"I interrupted you, Buck. What were you saying? About us working together?"

He checked the mirror again. "Like I said, if we work

together, maybe we can make them see how foolish this whole marriage thing is at their age."

"It's more than their age. Mom will be giving up her home in Kansas City, the home she shared with my father for over twenty-five years, to move—"

"Whoa, little lady. My father doesn't exactly live in an igloo. That lodge of ours is pretty nice."

Victoria twisted in the seat belt. "I didn't mean your father's place wasn't nice. It's just that Mom's the one who'll be making all the changes—new home, new friends, new surroundings. Looks to me like he's expecting her to give up everything while he's giving up nothing!"

Buck maneuvered the minivan around two cars and pulled in behind a truck loaded with logs. "What about his independence? His money? His freedom?"

"His independence? His money? His freedom?" Victoria echoed, finding it difficult to keep her voice down, as her blood pressure rose. "Seems to me she's giving up all of those and much more. I don't hear him volunteering to move to Kansas City!"

He seemed surprised. "Kansas City? Move from Alaska to Kansas City? Now why'd anyone want to do that?"

"Buck?" Ron reached over the seat back and rested his hand on his son's shoulder. "What's wrong?"

Buck sent a quick look at his companion. "Nothing, Dad. Victoria and I were just talking about—" He paused. "Alaska."

The elder man gave his son's shoulder a pat. "Good. Abigale and I want the two of you to get along." His other hand reached out and touched Victoria's shoulder. "After all, you're going to be kinfolk."

The young couple sat quietly, forcing smiles until Ron settled back in his seat and continued his conversation with Abigale.

"Kinfolk," Victoria muttered.

"Not if we work together. Look, Victoria, I don't like this

situation any better than you do."

She had to agree. Neither of them wanted this marriage. Maybe if they worked together. . .

The car behind them honked several times, then whizzed past the minivan. Buck hit the brakes and pulled quickly to the right, miraculously keeping the van under control. The four watched in horror as the offending car swerved into the lane in front of them, missing their front bumper by mere inches as the semi in the oncoming lane braked and pulled onto the paved shoulder. The car then swerved back to the left, nearly clipping the semi's back end before leveling out only a hair's width behind the log-laden semi in front of them.

Buck leaned on his horn, then shook his fist. "Stupid guy. That's how accidents happen! I hope he's ready to meet his Maker."

"That was close." Victoria took a deep breath and slumped back in the seat, trembling.

"Too close," Buck agreed, his eyes still riveted on the car ahead of him, anger blanketing his face.

Ron cradled Abigale in his arms. "Good defense driving, Son. Can you imagine a guy taking a chance like that? Where was his brain?"

"Sometimes people do stupid things without thinking them through!" Buck retorted.

Victoria winced. She was sure his answer had a double meaning. And as much as she wanted to turn and see if Ron and her mother had caught it too, she didn't.

❧

"Now that wasn't so bad, was it, Victoria?" Abigale asked as they stood in the lovely master bedroom at the Golden Nugget Lodge.

Victoria tossed her handbag onto the table. Then she plunked herself down beside her mother on the edge of the king-size bed. "Mom, it took us forever to get here! Do you realize how far we are from Kansas City? Have you even looked at a map?"

Abigale's eyes twinkled as she took her only daughter's hand in hers. "No, have you?"

Victoria had to admit she had no idea where Anchorage was located, only that it was in Alaska. She had long forgotten her geography lessons.

"Isn't this just the loveliest place you've ever seen, Honey? Those lush green pines, the flowers, the heavy timbers—"

"The long, dark winters, the wild animals, the isolation!" Victoria countered. "Mom! You'll die here."

Her mother laughed. "Don't you think that's a bit melodramatic? Die? I think not. I'm going to love it. Ron says—"

"Ron says! Ron says!" She pulled her hand away from her mother's grasp and stood. "You barely know the man, and you're talking like he knows you as well as—"

"As your father did? Oh, Victoria. Your father and I talked many times about doing something very much like this, when our children were all grown and out of the nest. We never had the money to take the adventurous trips we talked about, not when you kids were all at home. That's why we planned our anniversary trip. We wanted to do something totally different from the routine lifestyle of our forty-five-year marriage. We even talked about going to the Holy Land next year. And Africa the year after that, to visit those missionary friends of ours."

Victoria kicked off her shoes and sat down beside her mother again. "Really? Even Africa? You were both such homebodies."

"Just shows how little you really know me." She patted Victoria's cheek. "Some of us keep our dreams inside us. I guess because we fear we'll never have the opportunity to live them, and we don't want to be disappointed."

"But the trips you are talking about were visits. Marrying Ron Silverbow would mean living in Alaska. Permanently! That's a whole different thing."

ॠ

Abigale rose and walked to the bay window that overlooked the circle drive leading into the Golden Nugget Lodge. She watched Buck pulling their luggage from the open door at the back of his minivan and handing the bags to Ron, who placed them on the cart. The two men were so much alike it was uncanny. Both well over six feet and straight, despite Ron's additional years. Where Buck's shoulder-length hair was dark, Ron's was heavily peppered with silver. *If only Victoria could know the side of Ron I know. How can I explain this to my daughter? How can I tell her how lonely I've been since her father died? How can I reveal my fear of facing the future and old age without a husband by my side? And most of all, how can I convince her of my feelings of love for a man I met only a few days ago? I knew Ron and I were meant to be together the minute I saw him bow his head in prayer at our first meal together.*

Victoria followed her mother to the window. "Mom, look. I don't mean to be difficult. It's not that I don't want you to get married again. I'm sure Dad wouldn't want you to spend the rest of your life alone. But Alaska? With Ron Silverbow?"

"Victoria, I know you love me and want the best for me. But please, give Ron a chance. Get to know him. We have so much in common. He's a fine Christian man who loves God, like your father did." Her eyes misted over as she thought about her wonderful husband. "We'll be here most of the week, and I'm asking you, as a favor to me, try to keep an open mind. It may be difficult to believe, but Ron is everything I could want in a husband, and I want to marry him. Just try, please? For me?"

"Here's your luggage, ladies," Buck said. The two men, weighted down with suitcases, stood grinning in the doorway.

Buck pulled a face at their guests. "With all this stuff, you two could probably stay a month and never have to do laundry! Did you leave anything in your closets in Kansas City?"

ea

Ron placed his napkin on the table and leaned back in his chair. "That was a great dinner, Wasilla."

"Yes, sure was. And from the looks of Miss Victoria's empty plate, I'd say she enjoyed it too," Buck added. The woman with sleek black hair cleared the table.

Victoria shoved her plate away with a smile of contentment. "I didn't even know I liked salmon."

"I love fresh salmon," Abigale admitted. "We had some on the ship, and Ron told me about all the fresh salmon they serve here at the Golden Nugget dining room. They catch much of it themselves. Did you know that, Victoria?"

The young woman shrugged her shoulders with a slight smile. "Why am I not surprised?"

"When you come and visit your mom, Buck and I'll take you salmon fishing." Ron waved his empty coffee cup toward their waitress.

"Wasilla? That's your name?" Victoria asked as she held out her cup for a refill.

"Ask them two." The woman nodded.

Ron and Buck snickered.

"No. Her real name is too difficult to pronounce. She's from Wasilla, a little town down the road. Buck started calling her Wasilla the first day she hired on, and she's been Wasilla ever since," Ron said.

"How long have you worked here at the Lodge?" Abigale lifted her cup to her lips.

"Too long." Wasilla grinned.

Once the coffee was consumed and the dishes removed from the table, Ron took Abigale's hand in his and leaned toward her. "Sugar, how about taking a walk with me?"

Abigale nodded and the two took off, arm in arm, leaving Buck and Victoria seated at the table.

"You want to take a walk?" Buck asked.

Victoria stifled a little yawn. "Not me. I'm still on Kansas

City time. I think I'll turn in early if it's all right with you."

He nodded.

"Maybe I'll think better after a good night's sleep," Victoria said.

"Don't forget to pull down the blinds and close the drapes. It won't get dark until nearly two in the morning, and then it only gets to what you folks would call twilight. Makes it kind of hard to sleep when you're not used to it."

She grinned. "Thanks, I will."

"Plan on seeing the place in the morning. I'll be your guide."

"Sounds good. I hate to admit it, but this place is lovely. I'm anxious to see more. But you said you're a doctor. Don't you have to go to your office?"

"Not on Monday mornings." He fingered his thick mustache. "I only see patients in the afternoon on Mondays."

"Oh, I see. Did you have something else planned for tomorrow morning? We could take the tour later. I don't want to be a bother."

"No bother. I'm happy to show off the Lodge and the grounds."

Victoria was hoping a tour of the place would give her more ammunition to use in convincing Abigale that Ron was not the husband for her and Alaska was not the place for her to live.

"I think we've got our work cut out for us, Tori," Buck warned with a sigh. "Those two are gonna be hard to break up."

Tori? He called me Tori? No one has ever called me by that name.

"What do you think?" he added.

She traced the rim of the empty coffee cup with her fingertip. "Ah—I think you may be right. I tried to talk to my mom when we first got here, but you can chalk that conversation up to her side. I came out the loser."

"I know what you mean. I tried to talk to Dad when we

unloaded the luggage. I didn't have any success either."

"I'm at my wit's end. I'm wondering if I should call my brothers and ask them to come up and try to talk some sense into her."

Buck shook his head. "I'd hold off on that. You're only going to be here a week. It'll probably take them that long to get their affairs in order so they could be gone and get their airline tickets. Let's see what the two of us can do."

"So, what's the plan?"

Buck dipped his shoulders and stared at the ceiling. "I haven't a clue."

❧

Surprisingly, Victoria slept quite well and found herself rested and eager to meet the day when she awoke the next morning at eight, Alaskan time. After a hearty breakfast in the dining room with her mother, Victoria wandered around the lobby of the Lodge waiting for her guide. He arrived about nine and seemed surprised to see her ready to go.

"Did you think I'd sleep till noon?" She smiled. Without waiting for an answer, she added, "I'm ready for my tour. Are you sure you can spare the time this morning?"

Buck smiled and reached out his hand. She hesitated a bit, then took it.

"It's a great morning, I thought we'd walk. Is that okay with you?" He took a quick look at her feet.

"Wore my tennies," she quipped and stuck out one foot. "Lead on."

Victoria had been so weary and upset when they arrived the evening before she hadn't really noticed all the colorful flowers in full bloom around the Lodge's exterior. But now in the light of day, she was fully impressed with their beauty. "I've never seen such large geraniums!" She cupped a huge blossom between her hands. "How do you grow them like this?"

Buck broke off one of the larger red flowers and handed it to her. "We can't take all the credit. Over twenty years ago the city developed a program to put more blossoms and greenery around the area." He broke off a smaller white flower and sniffed it before handing it to her. "When we go into town, I'll show you the flowers they have along Fourth Avenue. They're part of that program. I think you'll be impressed."

Victoria lifted the white flower to her nose and inhaled deeply, taking in the sweet-smelling fragrance. "That's where you get these flowers?"

He laughed. "No, but once the Anchorage citizens started seeing the flowers around town, they all wanted some for their homes. So now we have huge commercial greenhouses that start the plants every year. In fact, during the dark days of winter, folks go up there just to sit on the wooden benches and enjoy the bright lights and the flowers. Then when it's warm enough, we all transplant them into our hanging baskets and gardens. With all the sun we have every day all summer, they grow pretty good."

"Pretty good? I'd call these more than pretty good. Folks back home would never believe the size of these flowers. And they're so healthy. Do you have a gardener to take care of them for you?"

Buck pulled his knife from the sheath on his belt and cut away a sagging branch on a small pine tree. "Gardener? No, not a regular one anyhow. We have a service that comes and plants them, but Dad and I do most of the upkeep of the baskets and gardens. Kind of a hobby with us."

Victoria eyed the flower-filled baskets hanging on a series of iron posts. The posts staked out the big circle drive leading to the Lodge's front door.

Buck folded his knife and slipped it into its sheath. "Like those posts, Tori? I welded them myself."

She turned quickly to face him. "What don't you do, Dr. Silverbow?"

With a shy grin as an answer, he took her hand and they began their walk. She couldn't believe the lushness of the trees and bushes, or the size of the Lodge as they circled its exterior. "How many rooms does the Golden Nugget have?"

He scratched his bearded chin. "Well, let me see, twenty on the first floor, twenty on the second, and ten cabins down by the creek. Plus Dad and Mom's suite." He looked embarrassed. "I mean—Dad's suite. Then we have the bunkhouse for the help. I reckon there's maybe sixteen or eighteen people living there during the busy season."

She frowned. "Where do you live? I assumed you lived at the Lodge."

He kicked a rock off the path with the toe of his worn boot. "Me? Live at the Lodge? No, I have my own place." He pointed up into the trees where you could barely see the tip of a roof peeking through. "Up there."

"I'm afraid my mother will find Alaska as beautiful as I'm finding it," Victoria confessed reluctantly. "I was hoping it'd be barren and ugly."

He stopped walking and picked up a chunk of wood from the path. "You fail geography?"

She laughed. "No, but I must have been absent when they studied the chapter on Alaska."

He motioned toward a little gazebo nestled in an overgrowth of trees, and they sat down on a weathered bench. "Alaska will grow on you if you give it a chance."

She watched as he again pulled his knife from its sheath and began to whittle on the chunk of wood he'd picked up. "But I don't want to give it a chance. Don't you understand? I want to take my mother and go home."

He sat silently. The only sound was the swoosh-swooshing of the blade as it made each cut.

Victoria bowed her head and folded her hands in her lap. "Ever since I was a senior in high school I've had plans to open my own gift shop. Now, just when we get the news our loan has been approved and we can go ahead with my dream, your dad comes along and rips it all apart."

"Well, I'd say your mother had an equal part in that rip, Tori. It takes two, you know."

She watched the chips fall away as he deftly moved the blade. "I know. It's not that I'm laying the whole blame on him—"

He looked up through dark, heavy brows. "Just the major part?"

"Not fair, huh?"

"Not quite. Let's blame them both."

She grinned.

"There." He brushed the chips from his lap and extended his hand toward her. "A flower for a lady." He placed a tiny carved blossom in her hand.

Her eyes widened with appreciation at his talent. In just a matter of minutes he'd carved what looked like a columbine blossom. "Buck, it's beautiful."

He grinned and placed the knife back in its sheath. "I like carving. It's my hobby."

"I'd like to see more of your carvings. Do you have any at the Lodge?"

"No. Most of my carvings are big. I'm talking huge. I carve totem poles."

"You mean real totem poles? Like ten feet high?"

"Some taller than that. They're a kind of therapy for me."

She looked puzzled. "Therapy?"

"Yeah." He glanced at his watch. "If you want, we can walk up to my place and I'll show you."

Ten minutes later, after a rather steep climb up a rocky path, they reached a slight clearing. Victoria caught her breath as she stared at the lovely house nestled into the thick foliage. "You live here?"

"Yes and no. It's my house. I lived here with my wife before. . ." His voice trailed off and he turned away from her. "I don't live here anymore. No one does. I live in the little bunk house over there." He pointed to a small cabin off to one side and slightly higher up than the house.

She wanted to ask more questions, but there was something in his tone that forbade it. When he offered his hand, she took it. They walked around the house and up the path to the bunkhouse.

"Sorry it's so messy up here," he apologized as they neared the cabin. "But the chips from my carvings make a good cover for the path. I just put them here rather than gather and burn them."

When they made the final turn, they were greeted by four magnificent totem poles, standing as if they were guarding the little cabin.

"You carved these?" Victoria asked, impressed with the detailed carving of the intricate yet grotesque faces staring down at her.

He nodded. "Yes, carved these a number of years ago, right after my wife and I were married. Up here in Alaska, totem poles have a special meaning. There's even a park dedicated to them here in Anchorage. Visitors come from all over the world to see them, even think of them as an art form."

Victoria glanced at the freshly cut chips that lay at their feet. "But you're still carving them, right?"

He seemed a little hesitant. "When I need to."

She didn't understand his answer. "When you need to? Do you sell them? Take custom orders?"

His face grew serious. "No. Never sell them."

She wanted to know more. "You're not working on one now?"

He swallowed hard, and even with his well-trimmed beard she could see his Adam's apple move. "Yes. Sort of."

"May—may I see it?"

He smoothed his mustache and appeared to be thinking over his answer. She wondered if her request had somehow invaded his privacy.

"Okay." He offered his hand once more and led her around

to the far side of the cabin. There on a stand made of two Xs lay a partially carved totem pole with the most grotesque faces she could imagine. Just the sight of them made her shudder, and she turned away.

"I know they're ugly. You don't have to tell me."

There was something so vulnerable in his voice. He was like a child who'd been caught stealing, or cheating on a test.

She mustered up her courage and asked, "But why? The others are like works of art. This one is—excuse me for saying it—hideous!"

He picked up a long-handled ax and gave a hearty swing at an uncarved section of the big pole. A huge chip flew through the air. "Remember I told you I use my carving for therapy? You have no idea how much frustration I can get rid of by cutting away at this awful thing."

He stepped back and held out the ax as he motioned toward the log. "Here, have a swing."

Her palm went to her chest as she backed away. "I couldn't. I might ruin something."

His laugh echoed through the hills. "Ruin it? That's impossible. The worse you can make it look, the better. Go ahead, give it a whack."

Reluctantly she took the ax. With both hands, she raised it high over her head and slammed the blade into the hard wood. A small, ragged chip joined his on the pile as she grinned awkwardly. "I guess I didn't hit it as hard as I thought I did."

"Good enough for a beginner, and you haven't had the practice I've had. But still, you have to admit it did feel good, didn't it?" He picked up a handful of chips and tossed them into the air with a hearty laugh.

But to her, his tone seemed sad. "Not really." She handed back the ax.

He took another huge swing, and the blade cut a second deep wedge into the seasoned wood. "I do this when I'm angry." He watched the chips fall onto the pile with the others.

"When you're angry?" Victoria asked. Her eyes grew round with question. "At who? Or what?"

Buck stared at her, and she almost wished she hadn't asked. She watched as he lifted a booted foot and let it rest on one of the crossbars that held the long pole. After a long, uncomfortable silence, he answered, "I've already told you. God."

four

"You mean because your wife and mother died?" Victoria asked.

Buck stood straight and tall, his face raised toward heaven, and his eyes took on an intensity that almost frightened her. "Exactly. He had no right to take them that way. Even if He was unhappy with me, He had no business taking Micah's mother and grandmother. And my dad sure didn't deserve to lose his wife. He's a good man."

"But," Victoria offered in feeble defense, "I'm sure it wasn't because He was unhappy with you. He had a plan—"

Buck swung around, his eyes blazing. "Don't give me that rot about His plan. If I've heard that excuse once, I've heard it a hundred times. That's what folks say when anyone dies. God had a plan." Buck's large hand tightly cupped her shoulder and she nearly winced. "A good God would not deliberately take a man's wife and a boy's mother."

"But did He?" She felt her voice wavering, her hurt and confusion welling up inside

"Did He what?" Buck's voice boomed. "Take her deliberately? Looks that way to me! You got another answer?"

She backed away slightly and Buck released his grasp. "No. I'm not the one to begin to explain God's plan to you. He failed me. . ." Her voice trailed off and she wished she had been silent.

Suddenly Buck seemed drawn back from his anger and into reality. "What'd you mean, failed you?"

Victoria knelt, picked up a handful of chips, and flung them into the air before answering. "I—He—I'd just as soon not talk about it."

"Got your own baggage, huh?"

She took a deep breath and let it out slowly. "Yeah, you might say that. But it all happened long ago."

A sympathetic smile tilted his lips. "Hate to tell you this, but it doesn't get any better with time."

"Tell me about it." Unwilling to tell more to this near stranger, Victoria turned and headed back down the path. "Our parents probably wonder where we are. Perhaps we'd better get back."

Buck picked up the ax. With one mighty swing, he nearly buried its head in the pole, and left it there. "Good idea."

෴

Abigale and Ron were sitting in the hotel dining room sipping coffee, giggling like two teenagers, Ron's fingers entwined across the table with his new fiancée's. "You two have a good walk?" Ron asked, rising long enough to greet them before sitting down and again twining his fingers with Abigale's.

"Nice. I never realized how beautiful Alaska is," Victoria conceded. She slipped out of her jacket and into the empty chair next to her mother.

Buck pulled off his jacket and seated himself opposite her. "All you need, Lady, is a good solid dose of northern exposure. And I intend to give it to you. I've arranged to go in a little late tomorrow morning. I'm going to take you on a tour of Anchorage, and I want to show you Cook's Inlet. And before you and your mom head back to the mainland, maybe Dad and I'll take you two up into the mountains."

"Look, Buck," Ron reminded him firmly, "Victoria may be going back to Kansas City but Abigale's here to stay. We *are* getting married, and don't you forget it."

Buck flashed his father a frown. "Aw, come on, Dad. You can't be serious."

"Serious as a heart attack, Bucky, my boy. And the sooner you realize it, the better." He signaled to Wasilla, and she hurried to their table. "Now, I suggest we all tell Wasilla what we'd like for lunch."

Buck glanced across the table to Victoria and shrugged. Although Victoria was glad the confrontation had stopped, she hoped his shrug didn't imply he was giving up. They had to change their parents' minds.

After they enjoyed a pleasant lunch of salmon salad, croissants, and a fresh fruit cup, Ron suggested Victoria and her mother spend some time together while the men folk took care of their chores. Abigale took her daughter's hand. They made their way up the dramatic, log-railed staircase to the second floor suite where Abigale was staying.

The rooms were beautifully decorated. Although Ron's deceased wife was not there, her presence was everywhere. Victoria sensed it the moment she entered. Abigale hurried to the massive stone fireplace and took down a large framed picture of Regina Silverbow. "Look, Victoria. Isn't she beautiful?"

The young woman stared at the picture. It was as though she were seeing a reflection of Buck in the woman's lovely face. The same dark eyes, the long sooty eyelashes, the dark wavy hair. She even had the same single dimple on her left cheek. The likeness was uncanny, and Victoria felt a twinge of sorrow pierce her gut. Each time Ron Silverbow looked at his son he had to be reminded of his wife. What agony that must be.

"Ronnie loved his wife. His life was centered around her," Abigale whispered somewhat wistfully. "He tells me he has never changed a thing in these rooms since her death. Even her clothes are still hanging in her closet."

Victoria placed the frame back on the mantel and dropped onto the sofa with a heavy heart. "Do you actually think you can take her place, Mom?"

Abigale sat down beside her. "I know I can. Ronnie has assured me of that. He said since Regina's death, many women have made a play for him. He jokes it's because he's one of Alaska's only two available males. Buck being the other."

"Well, it looks like none of them were able to capture him, Mom. What makes you think you're any different?"

Abigale pulled a lovely marquise diamond out of her pocket and placed it on the third finger of her left hand, next to the wedding ring Victoria's father had given her forty-five years ago. "Because of this. Ronnie and I went to the jeweler's this morning and picked it out. He wanted to place it on my finger, but I told him I wanted to talk to you first. Because once I take off your father's ring and Ronnie places his on my finger, I'm never taking it off again."

Tears flooded the young woman's eyes as she thought of her father and how happy her parents had been all those years they were together. "But, Mom—"

Abigale's fingers rose to touch her daughter's lips. "Shh, Victoria. I don't want to hear another word about this. My mind is made up. Just be assured that Ronnie and I discussed every bit of our lives during the seven days we had on that ship. Believe me, Honey, we know what we're doing."

"But Alaska is so far—"

"I know. But by plane, I'll only be a few hours away from you, and Ronnie has promised me I can go home for a visit whenever I want. And, of course, you and the rest of the family will always be welcome here anytime you can come."

Victoria bit her lip. She had so much to say—words she knew her mother didn't want to hear.

Abigale went on. "We're going to completely redo our living quarters here at the Lodge. Ronnie says I can do anything I want with this place. Change everything, if I desire." She moved to the fireplace and once again took down Regina's picture. "He even said we'd take down all of his wife's pictures and store them away." Abigale smiled and her fingers gently ran over the glass covering Regina Silverbow's likeness. "But I told him that was not necessary. I'm as happy that he shared that part of his life with such a wonderful woman as he is that I shared my life with a wonderful man.

Neither one of us ever wants to forget those precious times or the spouse we loved. Your father's pictures will go on the mantel right beside Regina's."

Victoria swallowed at a lump in her throat. It seemed Ron and her mother had discussed many more things than she'd realized. But the idea of losing her mother to Alaska and this man was no less agonizing.

"It seems you have your life with Ron all planned out, Mom, but what about my life? Have you so easily forgotten our plans? Yours and mine? Plans to open our gift shop? The shop we've been planning and working so hard to bring to fruition?"

Abigale placed Regina's picture back where it belonged and walked slowly toward her daughter, her face void of the smile. "That's the only hurdle I haven't been able to solve, Sweetie."

"How could you let me down this way, Mom? You know how much that shop means to me. It's been my dream since before my son was born. I'm an artist, Mom. I don't want to work for my brother the rest of my life. That's why I was so pleased when you agreed to be my business partner. You and I have taken the Better Business Bureau classes in preparation. We've researched a location. We've studied all the wholesale catalogues. We've done it all," The young woman paced across the floor, throwing her arms up in defeat. "And now, just like that," she snapped her fingers, "you're walking out on me? Right after the bank has agreed to give us our loan."

Abigale quickly rose to her feet. "I'm not walking out on you, Victoria."

Eyes flashing, the young woman turned to face her. "Then exactly what do you call it?"

"I'm marrying the man I love."

"Love? You call it love to marry a man you've only known seven days?"

Loving arms circled the young woman's shoulders. "I hate

to say this to you, Honey, but you've never known real love. It takes over your life. You have no other choice but to link up with the man God has sent to you. Remember what the Scriptures say? A man shall leave his father and mother and be joined to his wife?"

Victoria gave an indignant snort. "Where does it say you should leave your daughter and marry a second man? I've never read that in the Bible."

Abigale's face softened. "I want you and your brothers to understand, to realize I love Ron and want to become his wife. We don't know how many years we'll have together, but whatever amount we do have, we want to spend them with each other. Neither of us wants to be a burden to our children. When and if the time comes, we'll be there for one another, to care for each other. Yes, until death do us part."

"And what am I supposed to do?"

Abigale's arms tightened about Victoria's shoulders. Then Abigale kissed her daughter's cheek. "Be thankful your mother and Ron are both so happy, and go on with your life. You're young, you have a wonderful son, your brothers are all there for you in Kansas City, and the bank has approved our loan. It's all there for you. Reach out and grab your future with both hands."

Victoria pulled away. "The bank will never let me have the loan alone."

"They will if I'm your silent partner. Nothing has to change as far as they're concerned. As long as my name is on the dotted line and the monthly payments are made on time, they'll be quite happy."

Victoria was getting nowhere trying to talk her mother out of this ridiculous marriage. In fact, every argument she'd brought up against it, her mother had had an answer to defeat it. Perhaps, at this point, the best way to combat it was to let time take its course. Let her mother live in Alaska for a few days and see how different it is from Kansas City. Maybe as soon as the newness wore off and Ron Silverbow let his true self shine through, Abigale would see how very different the two of them were and come to her senses.

"I don't want to open this shop without you, Mother. If necessary I'll put off the opening and give you time to change your mind." Victoria straightened her shoulders, confident things would change.

"Don't count on it, Sweetie. I'm staying in Alaska as Ron's wife. Now you can either help me with my wedding plans or continue to sulk and try to upset me. Which is it going to be?"

"I'll try, but—"

"No buts, Victoria. I'm tired of hearing negatives."

"But the boys will be furious—"

"I'm sure, initially, your brothers will respond just as you have. But in the end, they'll want what's best for me. Once they meet Ron and see how in love we are, I'm confident they'll come around. Are you with me or against me?"

Victoria knew she was defeated. At least for now. "I'm with you, I guess."

"Good. Let's get started with the wedding plans."

Buck looked up from the computer. "Look, Dad. I know you're attracted to Abigale, any red-blooded man your age would be, but—"

"My age? You think my life is over, do you?"

The hinge on the computer chair squeaked as Buck leaned back and locked his hands behind his head. "You know I didn't mean it that way. You could probably take a man twenty years younger than you if you had a mind to."

"Well, then. What did you mean? That I'm too old to have another wife? You think I should spend the rest of my days living with the ghost of your mom? God rest her soul."

Buck considered his father's words. "No, I wouldn't expect you to do that. But what about all the women right here in Alaska, women that love the land like you do?"

"Easy to answer that one. I don't love any of them."

"But you think you love Abigale?"

Ron grinned as he leaned over Buck's shoulder and peered at the entries on the computer screen. "Nope, I don't think I love Abigale."

Buck brightened. "Good, I knew you'd come to your senses."

"Senses? That's not it at all. I don't *think* I love Abigale. I *know* I love Abigale!"

The chair squeaked once again as Buck leaped out of it and faced his father. "Dad! What has gotten into you? You've always been so levelheaded. How could you even consider such a foolish thing as marrying a woman from Kansas City? That woman has no idea what she is getting herself into. Do you think it's being fair to her, to convince her to pull up stakes and move to Alaska? Things are different up here. People are different. Life is different. What about the long, dark, cold winters? Do you think she can survive that?"

Ron twisted the tips of his graying mustache. "Son, I think you're the one who isn't thinking straight. I've worked hard all my life. I've made wise investments. I've been careful with my money. I'm not exactly poor. Actually, I think Abigale and I will enjoy those long, cold winters snuggling up by the fire, being with one another. But, if she gets cabin fever, we'll fly down to the Caribbean. Or spend time in Kansas City with her children. Or vacation in California. You're borrowing trouble, Son. We are more resilient than you think."

Buck shook his head woefully. "Is there anything I can say or do that will persuade you to put off this wedding for awhile? Give you time to reconsider your options? Make sure this woman is for you?"

Ron rose to his full six-foot-four. "Not a thing, Son. Not a thing. This old man is gonna marry Abigale Whitmore as soon as possible, with or without your consent."

"But, Dad—"

"Are you for me or against me?"

A deep sigh of defeat escaped Buck's lips. *Arguing is accomplishing nothing. Maybe time will work out things.* "With you, I guess."

❧

"Hey, Tori. Sleepyhead, you ready?" Buck yelled up the stairs early the next morning. I've got to be in my office by one o'clock. I have patients to see."

Victoria bounded down the staircase dressed in a red corduroy pantsuit, her long hair tied up in a ponytail and banded in red. "Sleepyhead? I've showered and had breakfast already." She smiled. "Where we off to?"

"That'd be telling. You'll just have to wait and see. Does your mom want to come with us?"

She stopped on the bottom step where she could look him eye to eye. "Mom? Go with us when she can stay here and make goo-goo eyes at your father? No way."

"Bat those baby blues, huh?" He grinned.

A few days before, Victoria would have been incensed at his comment, but not now. Now, although she would never admit it to Buck, she wondered if her mother *had* batted her baby blues at Ron on that ship. Otherwise, why would the man have fallen so deeply and so quickly in love with her? "Let's leave that remark alone," Victoria admonished. "We'll never know which one initiated the first flirtatious smile."

"You're right about that. I'm as surprised at my old man as you are at your mother. I'd have never guessed he'd do something so foolish. At his age!"

Victoria swept on past him with a flourish of her hand. "I hope I'm not that senile when I'm their age."

"Me either," Buck agreed as he turned to follow her. "Call your son?"

She nodded. "He's doing fine. He loves staying with my brother and his wife. They spoil him rotten."

"You actually have five brothers?" He opened the door and they stepped out into a beautiful, sunshiny morning.

"Yes, five. I'm the only girl. And the baby of the family."

Buck opened the door on the passenger side of the minivan. "I'll bet you are."

She scooted in. "Are you implying I'm spoiled?"

"I'm smarter than that." He winked, closed the door, and circled around to his side. Once inside the minivan, Buck said, "My mother didn't raise a dummy."

Victoria leaned against the headrest and folded her hands in her lap. "She must have been a lovely woman. Mom showed me her picture. You look just like her."

Buck inserted the key in the ignition and the minivan's engine roared. "I'll take that as a compliment."

"I meant it that way. Does your son look like her? By the way, when am I going to meet him?"

"He looks like me, so I guess he looks like her. Micah's been at a church retreat. He'll be home in a few days."

She frowned. "Church retreat? I—"

"You thought I was mad at God, right?" The car started down the hill and toward town.

She nodded.

"I am. But I've got a son to raise, and I figure being around church and church people won't hurt him. Raising kids alone is a tough proposition, and I need all the help I can get." He turned and gave a sheepish grin. "Guess you know all about that, you having a son and raising him alone."

"Yes, I do," she said simply.

"Well, I may be mad at God, but I know in my heart my wife would have wanted our son raised in the church. I guess folks around here don't know about God and me not being on speaking terms anymore. I put up a good front. And then there's my dad. He's one of those devout Christians, takes everything to God in prayer. You'd think he'd be mad at God too, after He took my mom like that."

"But he's not?"

Buck glanced in the rearview mirror, then made a left-hand turn. "Nope, not at all. Says it was God Who got him through the whole ordeal. Doesn't blame Him at all. Dad attends church and prays like nothing ever happened. Sits in the same pew he and my mom used to sit in. I think he finds comfort in it."

"Your father seems to be a good man. I'm glad to hear he goes to church regularly. So does my mom. I don't ever remember hearing her blame God for my father dying so young."

"You ever consider remarrying?"

His question came out of the blue and caught her off guard.

"I—no—it. . ." She stared out the window, avoiding his eyes.

"Hey, Tori. I get the feeling you're avoiding my questions—about your husband. Really, I don't mean to pry, but if we're going to be stepkin—"

She flung her head around, still reeling from his question. "But we're not going to be kin. Buck, we have to talk them out of this foolish marriage idea. For everyone's sake."

"I already tried and ran into a brick wall with the old guy. He's as bullheaded as that stubborn horse of his. I'm open to ideas if you got any." He waved at a passerby.

"I've tried too." She sounded defeated. "Mom is as stubborn as your dad. She even threatened me. Said I could either accept it and help her with her wedding plans, or continue to sulk and upset her. Didn't leave me much choice, did she?"

He offered a slight chuckle. "About as much as my dad offered me."

"Back to your question."

He frowned. "My question?"

"The one about me considering marrying again."

"Oh, that one. You don't have to answer, you know. I guess

I was prying into something that's none of my business."

She bit her lip. "Jonathan's father and I parted years ago."

Buck's eyes widened. "Oh?"

"I don't want to say anything more about it, Buck. I hope you understand."

He stared straight ahead. "Your privilege."

"I have considered marrying a man back home. Morton Pendergast. I've known him since I was a teenager. He's a few years older than me. Goes to our church. He has a very nice house, and a great job, and he thinks the world of Jonathan."

Buck's hand slipped over hers and he gave it a gentle squeeze. "But you don't love him, do you?"

Her eyes widened and she jerked her hand from his. "Why would you say that?"

"A woman in love doesn't talk about her man like that. Sounds like you're only considering marriage as a way to secure a good life for you and your son. I get the impression there's no love for the man."

Her eyes flashed with fire. "That's a rotten thing to say. You make me sound like a—"

He broke in. "A woman who'd say yes out of need?"

"I'd never do that!" Victoria retorted defensively.

"Well, you just said you were considering marrying the man, but not once have you mentioned love."

They rode along in silence, Victoria's heart pounding with outrage.

"I think I could love him," she confessed finally. "In time."

"That's a lousy way to start a marriage, Tori. I think we both know that."

She had to change the subject. He was getting much too close to reality. She was afraid in another two minutes she'd blurt out her life story, and she wasn't ready for that.

"Let's get back to our parents. How are we going to stop this wedding?" Victoria tried to make an unnoticeable dab at her eyes.

"Got me. But we have to find a way. And quick."

They spent the morning touring the city. Buck took her to the cultural sites and through the downtown area where she was able to admire the beautiful blue and yellow flower baskets hanging on all the light posts. Next, they went to the place where all the fishermen went to fish during the salmon run. They passed the statue of Captain Cook, and Buck took time to explain how Captain Cook was the same Captain Cook who explored the Antarctica and many other areas of the world. Eventually they ended up at Cook's Inlet.

"You don't ever want to go walking out there." Buck pointed to the rim of muck left along the edge by the low tide. "It's nearly high tide now. But when the tide goes out, the biggest part of this inlet is nothing but that heavy brown muck."

She frowned. "Why? From what I can see, it looks pretty solid."

"That's what many people think. When they get out there, their feet slowly start sinking. The first thing you know, it's too late and they can't get their feet out. One woman got stuck out there and by the time her husband got back to shore to get help, she was stuck so hard and so deep they couldn't pull her out. One of the firemen even tried to hold her up as he stood on a piece of plywood, but he couldn't. Eventually they had to leave her there when the water rose above her head."

Victoria shuddered. "How awful."

"Yeah," Buck agreed. "It was awful. Next morning a crowd gathered to watch as the water went down. And there she was."

"What a gruesome story."

Buck's arm circled her waist as they stood there. "It's part of Alaska, Tori. Like everywhere, we have the good, bad, and the ugly. That's the ugly."

"But why would she and her husband go out there?"

"People do it all the time. Finally, our fire department was able to get some special equipment that enables them to free people with a powerful hose that washes away the silt from around their feet and legs. Every year they rescue dozens of people."

"But there are warning signs everywhere." She turned and leaned into his chest, hating to even see the scene where such a tragedy could happen.

"We don't always heed the warning signs in life. That's what I'm afraid our parents are neglecting to do now. They're avoiding the warning signs. We have to make them see them, Tori. You and I. Will you help me?"

She looked up into his eyes and felt reassured. "Of course I'll help you."

He laughed. "Otherwise, you're going to have *six* brothers you know."

"We can't let that happen," she chortled. "Sometimes, five is four too many. And," she added as she slipped out of his arms, "you'd make an awful brother!"

"Yeah, but I'm a great doctor. And if I don't get to my office soon—"

Victoria turned and raced toward the minivan, calling back over her shoulder. "Beat you!"

Buck let her get a good head start, then darted after her, catching her just as she reached for the door handle, pulling her away. "You cheated. You had a head start."

"Did not," she told him, laughing and trying to catch her breath at the same time. "You're just slow, old man."

He pulled her to him and held her fast. "Old man, eh? I beat you, didn't I?"

"No, you didn't beat me."

"Okay, then, we tied. That satisfy you?"

She struggled to pull herself free, to no avail. "You're worse than a brother." She pushed him away.

"And you're too pretty to be any man's sister," he chided,

finally relaxing his grip. "But you'd make some man a great wife."

She grinned shyly. "Got anyone in mind? If the right man came along I might decide to stay in Alaska myself."

Buck winked. "I think you'll recognize him—when he comes along."

His words echoed in her mind all the way back to the hotel. Would she recognize true love when—and if—it came along? Hopefully, she'd have the opportunity to find out. Someday.

five

"We're no closer to breaking them up than we were two days ago," Victoria reminded Buck as they lingered over breakfast coffee. "In fact, if anything they're even closer."

He stared into his cup as Wasilla filled it to the brim. "All that lovey-dovey stuff almost makes me sick. I wonder if I was ever that foolish when my wife and I were courting."

"I—" Victoria stopped and her face took on a slight flush.

"You what?" Buck questioned softly, apparently realizing the thoughts that had gone through her mind were private.

"I—" she began again. "I can remember when I was in college and dating a man. I thought I was in love. I was even more foolish than my mother."

"Jonathan's father?"

She lowered her head and stirred at her coffee, which contained neither sugar nor cream. "Yes, Jonathan's father. I was sure I was in love with him and he with me."

"But he wasn't?"

"No. And now I can see that even with me it was infatuation. I was in awe of one of the big football players showing an interest in little old me, a mere freshman. A gullible, misguided freshman. He broke my heart."

His hand slipped across the table and circled hers. "I'm sorry, Tori. Honest I am. Some guys were born jerks."

She tried, but she couldn't stop the tear that wound its way down her cheek. "Like I said. It was a long time ago."

Buck's grip tightened on her hand as his other hand found its way to cup her chin and lift her face to meet his. "But you're still suffering from the unhappiness he caused, aren't you?"

She nodded and began to weep openly. Buck scooted across

to the chair next to hers and wrapped her in his arms, cradling her head against his shoulder. "Let it out, Tori. It's not good to hold something inside for so long. Go ahead, cry."

His voice was gentle, his concern so genuine, she found herself leaning into him and crying as if her heart would burst unless it found relief.

After she had had a good cry, she lifted watery eyes and found a look of compassion she never expected. Even though he didn't know her story, she felt as if he understood her misery. She was grateful. Back home in Kansas City, Victoria found it impossible to open up to anyone, even her mother, about the hurt and abandonment she felt when she gave birth to Jonathan and left the birth certificate blank where she should have listed the father. Instead, Victoria had put up a brave front and tried to let people think it didn't matter, claiming many single women gave birth to children every day. But in her heart, she wished there'd been another way. Oh, there'd been the abortion choice, but she couldn't do that.

"Sometimes life's the pits," Buck whispered. He pulled a red bandana from his pocket and wiped her tears.

"Yes, it is."

"Well, I'm here for you, Tori." He wrapped her securely in his arms. "You can count on me. I'd never let you down."

And she knew he meant those words. She'd come to greatly respect Buck in the short time she'd known him.

He wiped her tears again, then slipped back over into his chair. "I've got to go into the office early this morning and will be there most of the day. My patients are expecting me. What are your plans?"

She swallowed hard and fought to gather her wits, glad for a chance to put Armando out of her mind and get on to other things. "Gonna go shopping with Mother—for the wedding," she said without enthusiasm.

Buck became serious. "You know, Tori, I've been watching my dad and Abigale pretty closely these past few days, and I'm not sure we're doing the right thing trying to break them up."

She jumped to her feet, her hands on her hips as she glared at him, finding it difficult to believe she'd heard him right. "What? How can you say that, Buck?"

He took her hand in his, as if to calm her down. "Hold it, Tori. Let me have my say before you take me on. I'm beginning to think our parents are in love and just might make it together."

The room became icy silent as she continued to stare at this man whom she'd come to think of as her friend and ally.

"I mean it. My father has tried to convince me they can make it work, and I almost believe him. I haven't seen him this happy since Mom died. And since in a way it was my fault he lost her, who am I to try to take your mother away from him?"

Her arms crossed over her chest defensively. "So—out of guilt—you are asking me to sacrifice my mother to soothe your father's sorrow?"

"I wouldn't put it that way. But face it, your mom loves my dad. It's written all over her face. I honestly think they can make a great life together," he argued.

"And live in Alaska?" she asked snidely.

He nodded. "Yes, in Alaska."

"Even when it's dark twenty-four hours a day? And cold? And snow is up to the roof?"

"Come on, Tori. You know that's an exaggeration; it never gets that high." His lips formed a teasing grin. "Well, not often anyway."

She plopped into her chair and downed the last swig of coffee that'd been left in her cup, not even noticing it was cold. "I never thought I'd hear this coming from you, Buck Silverbow. I thought we were in agreement that we should do all we could to break them up before they did something foolish."

"Well, we'll have to finish this conversation later. My first patient is due in ten minutes, and I have a reputation of being on time."

Victoria watched as Buck took his last bite of toast, then pulled on his jacket. Even Buck had turned against her. It was beginning to seem as if marriage between Ron and her mother was inevitable. Victoria felt totally helpless. The only place she knew to turn was to God. But would He hear her after all these months she'd ignored Him?

"Morning, Sweetie," Abigale's voice sang out as she entered the dining room. "Sleep well?"

"Sleep? Knowing my mother is going to marry a man she barely knows and stay in Alaska? Sure, sleep came easily, about as easily as an A did in my college finals."

Abigale poured herself a cup of hot, steaming coffee and seated herself beside her daughter. "Wow, a little testy this morning, aren't we?"

Victoria decided to give it one more shot. "Why don't you give up this foolish dream and go home with me, Mom? Surely you've realized by this time marrying Ron would be a mistake. Admit it. No one back home has even heard what you planned to do. I'm the only one who knows, and I promise I'll never remind you of it again once we're back in Kansas City where we belong."

Abigale blew into her cup and sipped her coffee. "I'm going to forget you said that, Dear. I know this is hard for you to believe, but I do love Ron and I want to spend the rest of my life with him—in Alaska. And since we've been here nearly a week, Ron and I have decided it's time for us to go back to Kansas City and tell the boys and their families. He's made plane reservations for us for six tomorrow morning, so you'd better get a good night's sleep tonight. We're going home."

"But—"

Her mother lifted her hand. "No more, Victoria. It's settled, and you'd best get used to it."

"Micah's here!" Buck's voice ricocheted through the

lobby. "Victoria, Abigale, come and meet my son."

Victoria and her mother hurried across the now empty dining room, anxious to meet the boy his father had talked so much about.

"Micah, this is Mrs. Whitmore. She and your grandfather have decided to get married. She'll be your new grandmother."

Although noticeably surprised by his father's announcement, Micah reached out and vigorously shook Abigale's hand. "N–nice to meet you."

"And this is Victoria, her daughter. She'll be my stepsister, so I guess that'll make her your aunt. And she has a son just a year or two younger than you. You'll finally have a cousin."

Victoria wanted to scream. Everyone was being so cordial. Well, they might want this union, but she sure didn't, and she would do everything in her power to stop it. And she was sure once she was back in Kansas City, she'd have plenty of help. Her brothers would never stand for such a ridiculous marriage. Maybe her mother would respect their feelings about this more than she did her only daughter's. For the young boy's sake, Victoria put on her best face, masking the feelings that were tearing at her heart. "Hello, Micah. Your father has told me all about you. He's very proud of you."

"Thank you, Ma'am." The boy smiled toward his dad. Victoria was surprised by Micah's well-mannered behavior.

That evening, the entire group settled in the comfortable lobby area and visited for nearly an hour. Finally, it was Ron who stretched and yawned as he said, "Well, it's nearly nine o'clock. If we're going to catch that six o'clock flight in the morning we'd best hit the hay."

"Wish you could come with us, Buck," Abigale said as the group started up the steps.

"I tried to talk him into it, but he says he can't get away from his clinic," Ron answered, a sad note to his voice.

"I'm so anxious for you to meet my sons," Abigale added. "And for them to meet you."

"Guess you'll have to meet them in two weeks when they come for the wedding." Ron's arm found its way around Abigale's waist.

Victoria listened, but she wasn't happy. All this talk about meeting family members infuriated her. After her mother went into the suite where they were staying, Victoria hesitated in the hallway. With one final look toward Buck, she said, "Well, guess we won't be seeing one another again. Once my brothers get hold of my mother, the wedding will be off, I can assure you. Up here, I've been the only sane voice. But once we reach Kansas City, there'll be eleven of us to open Mother's eyes. Me, my brothers, and my brothers' wives. So don't rent a tuxedo, Buck. You won't get a chance to wear it."

Buck leaned toward her, his hand resting on the wall, his face so close she could feel the warmth of his breath on her cheek. "Don't count on it, Tori. You can't fight true love." And with that he planted a brotherly kiss on her cheek.

She ducked under his arm and opened the door, turning only long enough to say, "Good-bye, Buck. It's been swell." But the remembrance of that kiss lingered on her mind all night.

☙

Early the next morning, Buck drove the group to the airport. Victoria avoided eye contact with him, although she rode in the front seat with him. Their conversation was friendly but strained. She wished they could part under better terms; but since Buck had taken his father's side, that was impossible.

"Dad, you take Abigale and Victoria into the lobby, and I'll get a porter to bring in the luggage," Buck instructed once they'd reached the unloading area. "I'll park the minivan and join you in a few minutes. I'll meet you at your gate."

Ron nodded. "Okay, Son. But hurry. We'll want to say our good-byes before we leave."

Buck grinned. "I'll be there in plenty of time."

The three made their way to the ticket counter, and soon the porter appeared with their luggage. After producing their drivers' licenses and getting their boarding passes and instructions, the three headed to the appointed gate and seated themselves in a corner of the waiting area.

"Plane's on time," Ron told them after checking the big board that listed the departing flights. He glanced at his watch. "Wonder what's keeping Buck?"

"I'm sure he'll be here in plenty of time, Ron. Our plane doesn't leave for nearly a half hour."

"But they'll be calling for us to board any time now," Ron reminded her. "I wouldn't want to leave without seeing him."

"Flight Number 333 now boarding at gate 12 for Chicago," a voice boomed from a speaker. "Will all passengers please present your boarding passes at the gate for immediate boarding."

Ron scanned the area. "Where's Buck?"

"Probably got tied up in the parking lot," Victoria said, as she slipped an arm about her mother. She was feeling a little sad that she wouldn't have the opportunity to see Buck one more time and feeling a little guilty at the way she'd treated him the night before.

"Hey, you'd better get on board, I heard them call your flight," a familiar voice said as the three turned to see Buck hurrying toward them.

"Couldn't leave without saying good-bye." Ron reached out to hug his son.

"No need for that," Buck returned with a broad smile. "I'm going with you."

Victoria couldn't believe what she was hearing. "But you said you couldn't get away. How—?"

"Called old Doc Richards and talked him into coming out of retirement long enough to cover for me while I'm gone. The patients will love him."

"Oh, Buck. I'm so glad," Abigale said, reaching out to pat his hand. "Your father so wanted you to go."

"And you, Tori? How do you feel about me going?"

"Outnumbered," she answered, afraid of the influence Buck

might be on her brothers. "Why didn't you tell us last night?"

He grinned as he took her arm and hurried to catch up with their parents who had already disappeared into the skyway. "Didn't know then. Old Doc Richards was at a concert and I couldn't reach him until nearly ten, and by then you were asleep. I called, got my ticket, and here I am. Micah was invited to stay with a friend, so he's happy as well."

Victoria smiled despite herself. It was nice to have Buck by her side.

Eleven sets of eyes trained on the four people walking two by two through the doorway as the Whitmore men and their wives waited for their mother and sister.

"Mom!" It was Sam, Abigale's eldest son, and with him was Jonathan.

"Oh, come here." Victoria rushed to hug her son.

Abigale grabbed Ron's hand and hurried toward Sam, her arm outstretched. "Oh, Sam. This is Ron. I've told him all about you. And that's Buck, Ron's son."

Sam frowned. "Ah—nice to meet you, Ron," he murmured as if confused as to who Ron might be, then bent to kiss his mother's cheek. "And Buck."

Abigale kissed each son and daughter-in-law, telling each one, "This is Ron. And that is Buck."

After she greeted each one, Victoria could stand it no longer and spoke up loudly. "Mother, don't you think it's about time you told them who Ron is?"

All eyes riveted on the lovely gray-haired woman in the black pantsuit who was positively glowing. Abigale's eyes brightened with excitement as she leaned into Ron's side and laid her head against his broad shoulder. "Ron and I are going to be married. In Alaska, two weeks from today. And we want you all to come!"

It was as if every passenger in the crowded area became part of the Whitmore-Silverbow family as the area suddenly became silent and everyone turned toward the happy couple. The Whitmore men stood staring at their mother.

Sam finally spoke. "Is this some sort of joke?"

"No, it's true," Abigale decreed joyfully. "We met on the cruise ship and fell in love. I'm going to be Ron's wife. See?" She held out her left hand, the marquise diamond sparkling in the light.

Sam turned to his sister. "Victoria, what's going on here?"

Victoria shrugged, her arms still wrapped around her son. "You got me. I've been trying to talk her out of this for a week, but she's determined. I'm hoping you and the other boys will have more influence than I have."

Abigale stood proud and tall, looking much younger than her sixty-two years. "Look here, all of you, I'm your mother and quite old enough to make up my own mind about my life. You can accept my decision and be happy for me, or you can fight me and we'll all be miserable. Right now, all I want to do is get home and have a hot bath and a nap. My body is still on Alaskan time. If someone would be good enough to help us with our bags at baggage claim and show us to a car, we'll be on our way."

Five men nodded silently and followed their mother and her group to baggage claim.

Buck tapped his father on the shoulder as they stood waiting for their bags to arrive on the carousel. "Looks like you've got a tough bunch to convince."

Ron turned to face his son. "No convincing to do, Son. Abigale has already made up her mind. They either accept it, or they don't."

≥●

The next day the family met again. It was Saturday, so the whole clan assembled for a welcome-home lunch at Sam's house, which was the largest and could accommodate the most people. After a barbecue of ribs and hamburgers, the group gathered in the family room, sending the children outside to play.

Sam, who seemed to have been appointed by the others as spokesperson, looked at Ron as Abigale sat on the sofa entwined in Ron's long arms. "All of this came as quite a surprise to our family, Mr. Silverbow. I'm sure you can appreciate the predicament this puts us in. We love our mother and want the best for her. And—" He paused. "And we're just not sure marrying you and moving off to Alaska is the best thing."

Ron's voice was sure and confident. "I can understand every word you're saying, Sam. If I were in your shoes, I'd feel the very same way. But let me assure you that I, too, want what is best for your mother. And I intend to do everything in my power to provide that best for her—financially, spiritually, materially, and with more love than you could possibly imagine."

His words hung in the air, as each family member seemed to assess the words.

"But Alaska—it's so—far," one brother said.

"And cold," another offered.

"You'll all be welcome to visit your mother and me whenever you want. And don't worry about your mother." He gave Abigale a wink. "I'll keep her warm, I promise."

"But we'll all miss her," a daughter in law said. "We usually see her every day or so."

Ron grinned, his handsome face filled with the love he felt for Abigale. "My little sweetie can phone you as often as she likes. I promise to never complain about the phone bill. Whatever makes Abigale happy makes me happy."

"But—" Jason, the next eldest, began as he gestured toward his sister. "What about the gift shop you and Victoria were going to open? I got the bank to approve your loan."

His mother slipped her arm through Ron's. "We've already talked about that. I'll be Victoria's silent partner. That'll keep the bank happy, and she can go on with her plans."

Victoria broke her silence. "But it won't be the same without you. I'm not sure I can handle it by myself."

Abigale smiled toward her youngest child. "Of course you can, Dear. You're a smart woman, you can learn anything you need to. After a few months you'll have everything in hand, and you'll be glad you're running your own business by yourself, without me."

Sam spoke up. "We can all help Victoria, that's no problem. It seems to me the problem at hand is—will our mother be happy marrying again and living in Alaska?"

"*She* thinks so," Victoria said quickly, still hoping for a change of her mother's mind. "But I'm not so sure. It's different up there."

"Okay, Sis. You've been there, tell us about it. Have you seen where Mother will be living?" Jason asked.

She nodded. "Yes, I have."

"What's it like?" one of her sisters-in-law asked.

"Well, I have to admit it's beautiful where Ron's lodge is."

Sam broke in. "Ron's lodge? Explain."

Abigale's eyes sparkled. "Let me tell you. The Golden Nugget Lodge is quite large and very attractive. He has a wonderful staff working for him. It's surrounded by trees and loads of flowers, and the air is so clear you actually want to take deep breaths."

Everyone laughed.

"The nights are cool this time of year, but the sun is bright and warms both the earth and your spirit. Ronnie and I will be living in his suite on the second floor of the Lodge, and Ronnie wants me to redecorate the entire suite any way I choose." She gave them a sheepish grin. "And I won't even have to cook or do laundry, unless I want to. His staff will do all of that. Even clean our suite. So you see, I'll be just like a queen, living with my king." She reached upward, cupped Ron's chin with her hand, and kissed his cheek.

"Sounds good to me," Jason's wife said with a laugh. "Any vacancies in that lodge for our family?"

"Whenever you want to come. Just say the word and your

rooms will be ready," Ron said. "That's the advantage of owning a lodge. You always can make room for visiting relatives. And we both want you to come."

Victoria could feel her mother slipping away from her as one by one her brothers seemed to favorably consider their mother's announcement. "But you know Mom won't be happy living that far away from us. She's always lived in Kansas City, in the same house, for the past twenty-five years. You've got to talk her out of this." Victoria felt her voice quiver as she spoke, but she couldn't help it.

"Relax, Sis," Jason said with a reassuring smile. "We all want the best for Mom." He turned to Buck who had been silent. "How do you feel about all of this, Buck?"

Buck stood to his feet and surveyed the group seated in the family room. "Well, like Tori, at first I was as against it as she is. In fact, the two of us agreed to try and break up this pair." He glanced her way. "But after spending the week with your mom and my dad, and seeing them together and how happy they made one another, I kind of changed my mind. I'd like to see them get married, if they want to. They have my blessing."

Victoria glared at Buck. *Traitor*, she thought.

Abigale pulled away from Ron and walked to the center of the group, turning slowly, eyeing each person. "You know, you're all talking about me as if I weren't even here. Or worse than that—a senile old woman who doesn't know her mind. Well, family, let me assure you neither of those things are true. I'm sixty-two years old, fit as a fiddle, mentally alert, financially stable, and in love. I don't need your permission to marry Ronnie, although I prefer to have your blessing, even as Buck has given his. Now, go into a pow-wow or whatever you want to do. Ronnie and I are leaving. I want to take him to your father's grave and introduce them to one another." She turned to Victoria. "I'll see you and Buck at home later." Abigale took Ron's hand and they slipped out the door, leaving a befuddled family.

"Well, I guess your mother set that record straight," Jason's wife said quickly. "What are we all going to do about this?"

Buck stood to his feet again. "I feel like the fifth wheel in all of this. If you don't mind, Tori, I'll take your car and go on to your mom's house while you all talk."

"You don't need to leave, Buck," Sam responded with a warm smile. "You have as much stock in this as we do."

"Thanks, Sam, but if it's all the same to you, I'd rather bow out. I've already said my piece."

"I'm ready to cast my vote right now," Jason said. "For months I've watched Mother go downhill. Since Dad's death she's been like a hermit, walled up in that house of hers. It's been years since I can remember seeing her this happy. She's like a schoolgirl. I know Alaska is a long way away, but like Ron said, we can visit her anytime we like and she's only a phone call away. I hate to lose her as much as you all do, but can we be selfish enough to keep her from marrying Ron, if she loves him the way she says she does? Looks to me like he's a good man. I can't blame them for wanting to spend the rest of their years together."

Sam stood to his feet. "I agree with Jason. This has come as a shock, but to refuse to give our blessing would be pure selfishness on our part."

In turn, the other three brothers rose to their feet, voiced their opinions, and all agreed with Sam and Jason.

"Well, it looks like we're all in agreement. Let's tell Mom," Sam said proudly as he looked from one brother to the next.

"Oh, no you don't!" Victoria shouted, jumping to her feet. "I don't agree. I think it's wrong to encourage Mom to move to Alaska!"

Jason pointed his finger at his sister. "Sorry, Victoria. You're outnumbered. We all understand your feelings, you're Mom's only daughter. But majority rules."

Victoria spun around, grabbed Jonathan's hand, and headed toward the door, her face etched with anger. "I thought I could count on all of you to do the right thing. But you've all let me down. Buck included."

"You're getting your shop, Sis. What more do you want?" Sam asked, his fingers drumming the table, his impatience with his sister showing.

"You may forsake her, but I'm not. The shop can wait. If Mom goes to Alaska, I'm going with her. And I'm not leaving until I'm sure she's happy living there."

"You're going back to Alaska?" Jason's wife asked as she shifted her baby to her shoulder.

"You bet I am." Victoria jerked open the door, then turned to Buck. "You can ride home with Sam. Jonathan and I are going over to Morton's."

With a shrug of his shoulders and a quick smile toward the family he'd just met, Buck nodded. "Fine with me. I'll just stay here and get better acquainted with these good folks. Seems like we're all going to be related."

six

Victoria kept her distance on the night flight back to Alaska. It was dark, and since most of the passengers slept, there was little excuse for talking. She was glad she and Jonathan were seated across the aisle from Buck, Ron, and her mother. It made it easier to ignore them. Victoria was still upset with her brothers. Was she the only one who sensed impending doom for their mother's marriage?

She and Jonathan chattered on endlessly from the mini-van's backseat as she pointed out various sights along the way to the Lodge from the airport, sites she'd visited with Buck only days before. When they reached the Lodge, Micah was waiting in the doorway and hurried out to meet them.

"Jonathan, I want you to meet my son Micah," Buck said proudly. "I think you boys are going to be good friends."

"Want to see my knife?" Micah asked, his eyes shining with little-boy excitement. "My dad got it for me."

"Sure," Jonathan answered quickly, his eyes round with curiosity.

"Knife?" Victoria moved forward quickly, latching onto her son's arm. "Jonathan doesn't play with knives."

"They'll be fine, Tori. Kids in Alaska grow up with knives. Micah knows better than to take his knife out of its sheath unless I'm with him. Give the boy some space."

"Just make sure you don't touch it, Jonathan." She released her grip slowly. Perhaps she was being a little overprotective. Everyone told her so. Even her father had said she coddled her son.

The two boys ran through the lobby.

Buck grinned. "Boys."

"I don't know about the rest of you, but I'd like to take a shower and a nap." Abigale yawned. "Sleeping on a plane doesn't give much rest."

Ron patted her hand. "Now you go on up to your room, my little sweetie, and get your shower. I'll have your bags up in a jiffy."

Buck looked toward Victoria. "You look like you could use a nap too."

She bristled at the suggestion. "I slept on the plane."

"You never told me how your visit with old Morton came out."

She leaned against the desk and crossed her arms. "Didn't know I was supposed to tell you."

"He still after you to marry him?"

She nodded.

"Bet he was thrilled when he heard you were coming back up here to stay."

Victoria glared at Buck. "Not to stay, Buck. I'll only be here until I'm sure my mother is happy, or better yet, until she comes to her senses and decides to go back with me."

"You think you could be happy?"

She frowned. "Taking my mother home? Of course."

He shook his head. "No, I mean being married to Morton Pendergast."

"Of course I could. He's a fine man."

"But you don't love him."

"How do you know?"

"You can't fool me, Tori. A woman in love doesn't talk about her man the way you talk about Morton. Did he kiss you when you went to see him?"

Again, she bristled. "Of course he did."

With a mischievous grin, he moved right up into her face. "Like this?" He gave her a slight peck on the cheek.

She blushed but didn't answer.

"Or was it like this?" He quickly took her in his arms and

planted a deep lingering kiss on her lips.

She tried to pull away, but he wouldn't let her.

"Let me go." She pushed against his chest and tried to free herself. "What do you think you're doing?"

Buck let loose with a robust laugh. "Just trying to show you how people in love kiss. Hey, Tori, bet old Morton didn't kiss you like that."

She ran the back of her hand over her mouth. "Did too."

"Liar."

"You—you make me so mad—I'd—I'd like to—"

"Kiss me back?" Buck smiled.

Ron came in carrying his and Abigale's bags. "Buck, what are you two doing? Victoria looks like she'd like to take a swing at you."

"We're just having a little fun, Dad. Nothing serious going on, is there, Tori?"

Knowing nothing would be gained by complaining to Ron about his grown son, Victoria mustered up a fake smile. "Yeah, fun. Nothing serious that I can't handle."

"Good. I'd hate to have any hard feelings between you two." Ron headed for the stairway, whistling as he went, then called out over his shoulder as he reached the landing. "Because in just two weeks you'll be related. Brother and sister."

"Guess I'd better get the rest of the bags," Buck said. His finger reached out and touched the tip of Victoria's nose. "Go take a nap. You're gonna need your strength."

❧

During the next ten days Victoria saw very little of Buck. He had his patients to take care of and spent long days at his clinic and several late nights at the hospital with accident victims. She and her mother shopped, met with the pastor, the caterer, the florist, and everyone else it would take to pull off the wedding she and her husband-to-be wanted. Ron had encouraged Abigale to wear the wedding gown she'd worn when she married Victoria's father, which greatly pleased Abigale. At first the idea upset Victoria, but after talking to her mother and seeing how happy she was with her decision, Victoria resigned herself to it.

Ron was busy running the Lodge, and Micah and Jonathan were occupied playing with the myriad electronic toys Buck had bought for Micah, or exploring the foothills around the Lodge. It seemed everyone was busy—and happy—about the upcoming wedding. Except Victoria. And each day, as the wedding drew nearer, she became more depressed.

Finally, the big day arrived. Victoria's brothers had all arrived along with their wives and many children, and along with them came Morton Pendergast and several other close friends of the family. Ron had reserved plenty of rooms at the Lodge for all their guests and even had special tables reserved for them in the dining room for all their meals.

❧

"This is some place your father has here," Morton told Buck as the two men visited in the lobby. "Like Victoria, I'd sure never want to live in Alaska. But if I had to live here, this is the kind of place I'd want to live in. I hate cold weather and snow. I'd probably never leave that massive fireplace."

Buck smoothed his mustache, allowing his fingers to cover his smile of amusement. There wasn't much about Morton he liked. "I take it you don't ski. Or hunt."

"No!" Morton said. "I'm not much of a sportsman. And I could never slaughter an animal. Give me a good book and I'm happy."

"Victoria tells me you've never married. That so?"

"Absolutely. Never found a woman I'd want to marry. Until Victoria, that is."

Buck crossed his long legs, his weathered boots a sharp contrast to Morton's highly polished wing tips. "Oh? You're gonna marry her?"

"Well, she hasn't exactly said yes yet. But she will."

Buck hated the man's cockiness. "What makes you think so?"

Morton's fingers moved to check the knot on his silk designer tie. "I make a good living, have a beautiful home, and I can be a father to her son. And I'm a good catch. What more could a woman ask?"

"Something missing in that scenario, isn't there, Fellow?"

Morton appeared thoughtful. "Don't think so."

Buck squared his shoulders as he towered over the irritating little man in his Armani suit. Men like this drove him crazy. "How about love? I didn't hear you mention that word."

The man laughed, and Buck found him arrogant. "Love? A little old-fashioned, aren't you? You're forgetting Victoria and I aren't starry-eyed teenagers with raging hormones. I'm sure at this point in her life she's more interested in security and companionship than she is hearts and lace." He scrutinized Buck from head to toe. "Actually, you don't look like the romantic type. I'm surprised to hear you mention such things."

Buck settled back into the sofa's cushions, having a hard time understanding why this man he'd barely met aggravated him so. "Just goes to show you how looks can be deceiving."

"Well, take it from me, the last thing Victoria is interested in is romance. She's not the kind of woman who wants some guy hanging all over her."

Buck raised a brow. "How do you know? Have you tried it?"

The man's face flushed with anger or embarrassment. "Of course not. I'm a gentleman."

"Um." Buck stroked at his mustache again. "Gentlemen come in all types of packages."

"You two getting acquainted?" Victoria asked as she entered the lobby and seated herself beside Morton.

Buck stared at the two as they sat side by side. *If I were interested in that woman, I sure wouldn't take old Morton's approach. I'd show her what love is like—Alaskan style, and I don't mean rubbing noses.*

Victoria stood at the back of the chapel, her bouquet of white camellias held in her lace-gloved hand. She waited for the music to signal it was time for the wedding party to move down the long white carpet runner. She had to admit her mother never looked lovelier. Being engaged to Ron had taken years off Abigale's age. Despite her gray hair, she looked young, vital, and positively glowing. The wedding gown she'd worn forty-five years ago still fit perfectly. And although the white satin had turned to a cream color, it was as pretty now as it was in the photograph of her parents. Watching Abigale made Victoria's heart swell with pride.

And yet, her heart was also filled with sadness. And she wished she could turn the pages of time back to her freshman year. If she'd had her eyes open and hadn't been so enamored by Armando's good looks and popularity, her life might have turned out very differently. She might have married a nice boy and had a beautiful church wedding much like her mother's, rather than being a single mom raising a child by herself, without a husband or a wedding ring.

"Ready?" the handsome man in the black tuxedo standing beside her asked as he took her hand and tucked it into the crook of his arm. "Looks like the wedding is going to come off despite your efforts."

She gazed up into the sympathetic eyes of Buck Silverbow and returned his smile. "Seems I lost, doesn't it?"

He gave her hand a squeeze. "Well, she hasn't said I do yet. Want to give it another try?"

She gulped and then exhaled slowly. "No, I'll just tuck my tail between my legs and run away and hide once the ceremony's over."

He seemed surprised by her response. "Oh? That mean you're going back to Kansas and marry that stuffed shirt of yours?"

"I haven't decided."

"To marry him? Or to leave?"

The organ began to play, leaving both Victoria and Buck to wonder what her answer might have been.

The wedding party moved down the aisle and ended up at the flower-laden lattice arch at the front of the church. Buck gave his partner's hand a gentle squeeze and a quick wink as their hands separated. The pair moved to stand on either side of the arch, Buck by his father, and Victoria beside her son who held the heart-shaped pillow containing the wedding rings.

And then the bride appeared, her face vaguely covered by a fingertip veil of white illusion, which didn't even begin to mask her blissful smile. Victoria's heart leaped. Her mother was so radiant, so alive. Victoria felt a pang of jealousy. Why couldn't she find the same happiness her mother had found? Twice!

She caught a glimpse of Morton Pendergast and found him looking at her. She sent a weak smile his way. Would marriage to Morton be so bad? Couldn't she learn to love him, in time?

As she turned away from Morton and back to the happy couple, her eyes locked with Buck's and her heart seemed to skip a beat. But why?

As the vows were exchanged, Victoria found herself repeating them along with her mother, wondering all the while if she would ever have a chance to repeat them to the man she loved. A slight smile tilted at her lips. What man?

The soloist sang, the rings were exchanged, and soon the ceremony ended. Everyone was smiling and happy. Even Victoria felt the joy that permeated the air. In the revelry of the moment, she'd lost sight of Buck; but she knew he was more than okay with the way things had worked out for his father and Abigale.

A delicate hand clamped over her wrist. "It's over! I'm Mrs. Ronald Silverbow. Please be happy for me, Victoria."

Abigale's face beamed with delight.

Victoria forced a smile. "I am happy for you, Mom. I just hope you've—"

"Don't even say it, Sweetie. I don't want to hear any negative words. This is my wedding day!"

Her daughter donned her best smile, for her mother's sake. "You're right. You've chosen to marry Ron and live in Alaska. I guess I'll have to learn to live with it whether I like it or not." She planted a kiss on her mother's flushed cheek. "Congratulations, Mrs. Ronald Silverbow."

Abigale beamed. "I knew I could count on you." She began to search the crowd. "Do you know where Buck is? Ronnie's trying to find him. He seems to have disappeared."

Victoria scanned the crowd but Buck was nowhere to be found. "I haven't seen him since we left the chapel."

"Well, if you see him, tell him his father and his new stepmother are looking for him." Abigale's eyes sparkled as she lifted her bouquet. "Be sure you're there when I toss my bouquet, you just might be the one to catch it."

"I should be so lucky," Victoria mumbled as Ron whisked away Abigale.

The reception line formed and the wedding party began greeting the wedding attendees one by one—all but Buck. He seemed to have disappeared. No one knew where he was, not even Micah. Victoria kept an eye out for him but to no avail.

"Get ready," Abigale told all the women who'd gathered at the foot of the steps outside the church. "I'm going to toss the bouquet."

Victoria joined the group but felt nothing like catching her mother's bouquet, a constant reminder of her mother's decision to leave her and marry an Alaskan man. In fact, she was barely paying attention when the bouquet left her mother's hands and flew through the air and headed straight for Neva Wilson, the mother of six.

But instead of reaching up to catch the lovely camellias,

the woman ducked and the bouquet continued its flight and dropped into Victoria's hands. Aghast, Victoria hurriedly tried to hand it to one of the ladies standing near her, but they all refused.

"It's yours." Neva Wilson laughed. "You caught it fair and square."

"Looks like you're going to have to say yes to me after all," Morton said as he moved through the crowd and joined her. "Catching those flowers must be an omen." He took her hand in his. "What do you say? Will you marry me?"

Victoria stared at the man she'd known so long. She wondered, when Morton kissed her, why she felt different than when Buck kissed her. "I have too many things on my mind right now, Morton," she said, backing away from him. "We'll talk later. Right now I have something I have to take care of."

"Don't put me off too long, Victoria. There are plenty of other women out there who'd jump at the chance to marry me." His confidence irritated her.

Without answering, she headed for the little car Ron had rented for her to use during her stay in Anchorage.

She parked near the back door of the Lodge and took the path up the hill, struggling to hold up her long skirt to avoid tripping on the rocks as she moved. It was a beautiful day, much like a spring day in Kansas City. The sky was a clear blue with only a small occasional cloud.

Up ahead she caught sight of a tall male figure dressed in a black tuxedo, moving up the path a few minutes ahead of her. Sure he hadn't seen her, she hurried to catch him, the bouquet still clutched in her hand. By the time she reached the clearing, he'd seated himself on a fallen tree and was staring off in space, his black cummerbund dangling in his hand. Caught up in his thoughts, he didn't even notice her as she walked up to him. "Buck," she said softly.

He jumped and dabbed at his eyes with his sleeve. "What are you doing up here? I supposed you were still at the church."

"I—" Why had she come there? She wasn't sure herself. All she knew was that she wanted to find him. Right now, he was the only one who might understand her feelings. "I'm not really sure. Guess I wanted to escape. Guess you did too." She seated herself beside him and kicked off her shoes. "These aren't exactly for hiking. My feet hurt."

He laughed and she felt those butterflies again.

"You're right about the escaping. I did fine until they got to that 'death do us part' line. All I could think about was my own wedding and how beautiful Claudette was in her wedding gown. She looked like an angel." The laugh disappeared and an unsteady smile took its place.

"I'm sorry, Buck. I never thought—"

"It's okay. I don't say much about it to folks, but the hurt is still there. There's never a day goes by that I don't feel her presence near me." He gestured toward the home he'd built for Claudette, the one that had remained unoccupied since her death. "I come up here and talk to her. Foolish, huh?"

"No, not foolish at all! She was an important part of your life." Victoria wished she were gifted with words. Right now they seemed to fail her.

With the toe of his black leather boots, Buck kicked the wood chips that surrounded his feet. "Not a part of my life, Tori. She was my life! A part of me died when she did." The big man's hands flew to his face and he began to weep openly, his sobs racking at his chest.

Victoria wasn't sure exactly what she should do to comfort Buck. Finally, she gathered courage to slip her arms about his neck and cradle his head against her breast. Her fingers stroked his hair, much like she did Jonathan's when he needed comforting. "It's okay, Buck. Go ahead. Cry it out. It'll make you feel better."

He tried to pull away, but she held fast. When he relaxed a bit and his chest quit heaving, she lifted the hem of her long skirt and wiped his tears. The two were so close she could feel the beat of his heart as he agonized there beside her.

"You must think I'm a real pantywaist," he said softly. He sucked in a deep breath. "Macho men don't cry."

"They do if they've lost a loved one," she said, trying to console him. "I'd say it takes a real man to cry. You must have loved her deeply."

He pushed away a bit. "I did. Guess I still do. My biggest regret, other than for myself, is that Micah was so young when she left us. He barely remembers her."

"Have—have you ever considered marrying again?"

"No."

His answer was spoken with such firmness she wished she'd never asked.

"I'd never find another woman like Claudette. When she died, I told myself I'd never marry again. In fact, the day she was buried, I put my hand on her casket and promised her I'd never let another woman take her place."

"And you closed up your house?"

"Yes. I couldn't go back there to live without her."

"I think I can understand that."

"Most folks don't. Some think I'm crazy. Others have tried to set me up with some pretty, nice women, but I wouldn't have any part of it. I'd rather spend the rest of my life alone."

"Do you have a picture of her?"

A smile crept across his tear-stained face as he reached into his pocket for his wallet. "Oh, yes. Always carry one with me." He pulled the picture out and handed it to her.

"She's beautiful," Victoria said, meaning it. The woman staring back at her looked much like Buck. Same dark hair, dark eyes, and a smile almost as beautiful as his. "She looks enough like you to be your sister."

His grin shook up those butterflies once more. "That's what everyone used to say. Guess it's our genes. We both have Athabascan Indian ancestors."

Victoria's face sobered. "Honestly, Buck. I'm so sorry

about your wife. It must have been terrible losing her like that. And your mother too. I wish I'd have had a chance to meet them both. They must have been very special people."

"They were," he said with a note of overwhelming sadness as he took back the picture. After one last look, he placed it back in his wallet.

Victoria shivered and wrapped her arms about herself. Buck noticed and quickly tugged off his jacket. "Here, take this. Gets cool pretty quick once that sun goes down."

She backed away and held up a palm between them. "No, I couldn't. Besides, it's time I left you alone. I'm sure you didn't plan on having company when you came up here."

He slipped the jacket over her shoulders and pulled her back down beside him. "Please stay. I like having you here."

She knew she should go, but in her heart she wanted to stay. There was something so comforting about being near this man. Knowing he would be close to her mother in some way helped. It made leaving her in Alaska somewhat bearable. "If you're sure—"

"I'm sure. After all, you are my sister now." He slipped an arm about her waist and drew her close. "That better?"

She smiled. "Much better, thank you. But I don't want you getting cold."

He gave her a slight squeeze. "Hey, are you forgetting? Me tough Alaskan man!"

"Seriously, Buck. I don't know what to do about Mom."

He lifted a brow. "Not much you can do now—she's married."

Victoria leaned into him. His body made her feel warm and secure. "I know, Silly. I mean about leaving her. I'd vowed I would not leave until I was convinced she was happy living here."

"So, what's the problem? Don't leave."

She gave him a look of surprise. "You think I should stay?

Won't your father resent my presence?"

"Why should he? You heard him say whatever makes Abigale happy makes him happy. I'm sure she'd want you to stay as long as you'd like." Buck grinned. "And I would too. I've never had a sister before. I kind of like the idea. But what about that shop you were going to open?"

"I guess I could put it on hold."

"Good. So, do it."

A look of trouble clouded her face. "I'd have to get a job. I won't take charity. And Jonathan and I would have to have a place to live."

"Plenty of room at the Lodge. And I'm sure there are plenty of people who'd like to hire a good-looking, talented, smart girl like you."

"Flatterer. Seems you have all the answers."

"I also have a question."

"Oh?"

"What about old Morton?"

"Guess he'll have to wait until I make sure Mom's settled."

"Think he'll wait?"

"Morton? Oh, yes. He's a very patient man."

"I can think of a few other words to describe him. Stuffed shirt. Arrogant. Egotistical. Want to hear more?"

She shook her head and cocked a brow. "No, that's plenty. Why do I get the feeling you don't like him much?"

"Perceptive little thing, aren't you? I just don't happen to like men who think the world revolves around them."

She pursed her lips. "He's a good man, Buck. Jonathan and I would want for nothing if I married him."

"Except the thing you need the most."

"And just what is that?"

He stood awkwardly, shifting from one foot to the other before lifting his eyes to hers.

"Go on, you can tell me. I'm your sister, remember?"

"You're sure you want to hear this?"

"Yes. Say it. What is the one thing I'd be missing if I married Morton, Dr. Silverbow?"

Pulling himself up to his full six-foot-four, he answered with one word.

"Love."

seven

"Look, Victoria, I understand your concern for your mother, but don't you think you're being a bit foolish staying here in Alaska with her? Do you plan to go along on her honeymoon?" Morton Pendergast pulled a boarding pass from his coat pocket and waited for her answer.

"Morton, I have no intention of going on Mom's honeymoon with her. As a matter of fact, they're not going on a honeymoon. Not for awhile anyway. Ron wants to take Mom to the Caribbean when the Alaskan weather turns cold."

"Well, I'll ask you one more time. Come home with me and let's set a wedding date. I have an important convention coming up in France next spring, and it would help my professional image if I had an attractive wife to attend with me."

She frowned. "That's why you're asking me to marry you? For business reasons?"

"That's not the only reason, Victoria. You're pretty, you're smart, you're talented. You and I would make a great team," he stated without hesitation. "And think of all the social functions you'd be able to attend as my wife."

Victoria stared at him. She couldn't believe what she was hearing. Why was it each time she saw Morton now, Buck's words came back to her. Stuffed shirt. Arrogant. Egotistical. She'd never really thought of Morton that way before, but now that Morton had spelled out his reasons for wanting to marry her and Buck had called his ways to her attention, it was all she could think about when she was with him.

"I'm sorry, Morton. But for now, I'm putting my own life on hold. Perhaps after Mom is settled and I'm back in Kansas City, I'll—"

Morton tossed his jacket over his arm and picked up his briefcase. "Don't wait too long, Victoria. You'll never do any better than me, you know."

"So you've told me." Anger tainted her voice. "Have a pleasant flight."

Buck was climbing into the minivan when she arrived back at the Lodge. "Get old what's-his-name off okay?"

"Yes, he's gone."

"Good. Glad he's gone. I didn't like that guy." With that, Buck took off down the road toward the hospital.

Early the next morning after enrolling her son in school, and with the classified section of the newspaper under her arm, Victoria searched for a job. Several days of filling out forms and enduring endless interviews yielded nothing other than a few minimum-wage jobs, paying much less than she felt she and Jonathan could live on. She had her savings to fall back on, but that was earmarked for the new shop she planned to open back home.

"How's the job hunting going?" Buck asked at the dinner table one evening after a particularly frustrating day for Victoria.

"Not good. I thought I was preparing myself for a real world occupation when I majored in graphic arts. No one wants to hire me. I may end up having to go home after all."

"Aw, Mom. I don't want to go home," Jonathan complained. Wasilla poured him another glass of milk. "I like school and Micah, and Buck promised to take me and Micah to a ball game Saturday."

"If I don't find a job soon—"

"Now, Dear," Abigale said, laying down her fork, "I told you I'd help you out in any way I can. I still have the money your father left me and—"

Victoria shook her head. "No. If I can't make it on my own, I'm leaving. I'm not going to be a burden to anyone. I don't want to leave, but I may have no choice. I've made up my mind. If I don't have a job by this weekend, we're going home. It's time I stood on my own two feet."

That night as she made ready for bed, her eyes were drawn to the Gideon Bible on the nightstand. It'd been weeks since she had read a Bible, but tonight she felt the need to seek its comfort. Someone had placed a marker in the book of Philippians and had used a green highlighter to mark verse 19 of the fourth chapter. Victoria read aloud, "But my God shall supply all your need according to his riches in glory by Christ Jesus."

All my needs, God? Victoria's fingers traced the words. *I've been separated from You for a long time. But for my son's sake, for my mom's sake, if You want us to stay in Alaska, please provide me a job.*

❧

"Hey, Tori. You'll never guess what happened," Buck said as he arrived at the Lodge unexpectedly for lunch the next day. "When I got in the office this morning, my head nurse told me she and the others had decided to quit if I didn't hire someone to help get caught up in the office and to act as my assistant when we get overloaded with patients. It's only a temporary job. I told them I knew just the woman for the job. They want you to start tomorrow. Can you make it?"

She eyed him suspiciously. "Really, Buck? You're not just creating this position, are you? Do you really need someone?"

He let loose a robust laugh. Then he grabbed his napkin and spread it across his lap. "Hey, would I lie to my own little sister? Ask Dad. He knows how the women in my office are always grumbling about being overworked."

Ron tore himself away from his new bride long enough to answer. "He's right, Victoria. Complain, complain, complain. That's all they do."

"Well, if you're sure—"

"You bet I'm sure. Will you take the job or am I going to have to run an ad in the paper?"

"No! I'll take it, and thanks."

Buck raised a hand. "Don't thank me yet. You don't know what a tough taskmaster I am. I'm a bear to work for."

"A teddy bear." Ron winked at his son.

"You won't be sorry, Buck. I promise," Victoria said, relieved she didn't have to leave her mother yet.

"My pleasure," Buck said. "I like having you here."

෨

The next few weeks flew by. Jonathan loved his new school, he and Micah were inseparable, and Victoria was happy in her new job. She'd never realized how important Buck was to the community until each day she watched as he treated dozens of patients, some only with tender, kind words. His patience never ceased to amaze her. The man was tireless. She especially liked the way he was with the babies and young children. They all loved him and trusted him right from the start, letting him examine them and give them shots with little or no complaint. She was especially impressed when Jean, the head nurse, told her how many patients Buck treated who were never able to pay him.

"He sends them a bill marked paid in full. That's the kind of man he is," Jean told Victoria one day when they were having a late lunch together. "Never seen a man like him. He could be making good money in Vancouver or Seattle. But you think he's interested? No way. He's an Alaskan through and through."

As his assistant, Victoria learned much about Dr. Buck Silverbow. His kindness toward his elderly patients, his gentleness with those who were ill, his generosity to those who could not pay, his concern for those who were hurting—his virtues were endless. Victoria developed a high respect for him both as a man and as a doctor.

If I could ever learn to trust a man again, it would be a man like Buck Silverbow, she admitted to herself one night when she was with him at the hospital. She was assisting him with a man whose car had been sideswiped by a truck. Although Buck didn't say anything, Victoria was sure he was reliving his wife's accident. Buck did everything he could, but the man died. Victoria cried when she watched Buck's compassion as he told the man's family.

On the way home, Buck and Victoria stopped at an all-night café for coffee and rolls. Although their talk was light, inwardly each was filled with deep sorrow at the loss of their patient. Finally, Victoria could no longer stand the chitchat. "How do you do it, Buck? Day in and day out you're faced with misery and death, yet you seem to revel in being a doctor. The demands on you and your life are unbelievable."

His hands cupped hers. "Easy. I just look into their faces and see their pain and anguish. And knowing I might be able to help them gives me great gratification. I don't always succeed, but I know I've tried. I can't find words to describe it. I just know it fills me with satisfaction."

"I can see that. It's written all over your face. You're quite a man, Dr. Silverbow."

"Hey, you're gonna turn a guy's head. Let's change the subject. How about renting a movie tonight, something the boys will like? You can come up to the cabin and we'll pop it into the VCR."

"Great. I'm sure the kids will love it."

"Good. How about I have Wasilla box up a pizza for us, and we'll eat while we watch the movie? That way the boys can get to bed early."

"Terrific idea. Let's do it. I'll try to get back to the Lodge a little early and see if Wasilla will let me bake a batch of my famous peanut butter cookies."

Buck smiled. "You know how to cook?"

"A few things, but I'm best at baking sweets, of course."

❧

Victoria, Jonathan, and Micah enjoyed the movie, but Dr. Silverbow fell asleep as soon as he'd finished his pizza.

Victoria watched the sleeping man, his head pressed against the recliner back, his long legs dangling over the end of the footrest. She wondered what it would be like to be married to a man like Buck, living in a house with two sons, like normal married couples. Then she thought of Morton. Debonair, sophisticated Morton. Somehow he didn't fit into her picture of the perfect family. But Buck did.

The next few weeks Victoria was happy. In addition to spending time with her mother and new stepfather, she spent wonderful times as she joined Buck on his early morning walks before going into the clinic. One morning they met one of Buck's patients, a young woman pushing her baby in a stroller. Buck stopped to introduce them, then made baby sounds to the adorable baby girl all wrapped up in a pink snuggly. The baby smiled at Buck immediately and grasped his thumb.

"You have quite a way with children," Victoria told him as they made their way on up the path.

"Claudette and I had planned on having a house full of kids. I love them. At one time I even considered being a pediatrician. But how about you? You want more kids?"

She bit back feelings of hurt and disappointment, "Oh, yes. I'd love to have a little girl. When I was a child playing with dolls, I used to visualize having a little girl, tying bows in her hair and dressing her in frilly little dresses. But it looks like that'll never happen."

"Why not? Doesn't old Morton want kids?"

She could tell Buck was slowing his pace for her benefit. His long strides made it difficult to keep in step. "No, he doesn't. He's made that very clear to me. Although he's good to Jonathan, I think he only tolerates him because of me."

"And what does your son think about old Morton?"

She rolled her eyes. "He hates him."

"Ah, a perceptive kid." Buck winked and quickened his pace. "We'd better be heading back if we're going to get to the clinic on time."

The clinic was filled with patients when they arrived. Buck had a habit of allowing people to walk in without an appointment if they had a problem, and many of them seemed to abuse that privilege.

About ten o'clock a pregnant woman elbowed her way through the waiting room and demanded to see Dr. Silverbow immediately. Jean, the head nurse, seemed to know the woman and tried to calm her down. Victoria's efforts to calm the woman also failed.

Finally, in order to keep peace, Buck came into the waiting room. "Well, hello. We haven't seen you for a long time. I'm sorry I don't remember your name. What can I do for you?"

The woman waved her finger in his face as she patted her extended stomach. "You better remember me. You're the father of my baby!"

eight

Buck reeled backward. Those in the crowded waiting room fell silent as every eye zeroed in on Buck and the woman.

"Look, I don't know what your game is, but I'm certainly not that baby's father. Now, if you'll excuse me, I have patients to see." His voice was calm, but everyone could tell her words had upset him.

The woman grabbed his sleeve and pulled him around. "Oh, no you don't, I'm—"

"If you have something to say to me, I suggest you come into my office," Buck told her in a controlled voice. He motioned to Victoria. "And you come with us."

Victoria followed the two of them, her heart broken. The only man she'd ever felt she could trust had just been accused of fathering a child outside of marriage.

Buck motioned to the woman and Victoria to be seated, then circled his desk and dropped into the high-back leather chair. "Now, I don't even know your name."

"Bonnie. Bonnie Connor," she said simply, her hand still on her large stomach.

"How far along are you?" the ever-present doctor asked.

"A little over eight months."

"Have you been under a doctor's care?"

"No. I couldn't afford no doctor."

"Well, I will be glad to examine you and provide you with vitamins, free of charge. Or, I can recommend you to another doctor in the area. But—I am not that baby's father."

Victoria wanted to run, to get as far away from Buck as possible. There was no reason a woman would accuse a man of being the father of her baby if it weren't true. Especially if that man was nearly a stranger to her.

"Oh, yes you are," the woman said in a near scream. "Don't try to deny it. This is your baby and you're going to have to take care of it. I don't want no baby. Never did!"

Once again, in that calm voice that had come to irritate Victoria, Buck told the woman, "I am not the father, Bonnie. There is no way I could be. You and I have never been together except right here in this office, and I have a policy of never examining a woman patient without one of my nurses present." He rose to his feet. "Now, why don't you just go and we'll forget about this whole thing. I think you're just overwrought. You need to take care of both yourself and that baby. I'll have my nurse fix you up with some vitamins, and I suggest you take them regularly from now until time for the birth."

How can he be so matter-of-fact? Victoria asked herself as she watched the scene. *Either he's innocent or he's very good at covering up his actions.*

But the woman wasn't so easily appeased. "Either you admit your paternity, or I'm going to make sure everyone in Anchorage knows you're the father of my baby and you've refused to help me."

Buck had obviously had it. He took the woman by the arm and ushered her out of his office and out the side door. "Look, I'm not about to be conned. I don't know why you're doing this, but I am not the father of that child, and I refuse to take the responsibility for it. Tell anyone you want. If necessary, I'll meet you in court. Now, get out of here and don't come back!" Buck slammed the door.

"Are you?" Victoria asked, still not convinced the woman was lying.

Buck seemed surprised. "The father? Of course not. I can't believe you'd even consider that I am."

Victoria had to get away. After telling the head nurse she was leaving for the day, Victoria headed for the Lodge.

Fortunately, both Ron and Abigale were out, and she was able to go directly to her room without talking to anyone. Her tears were just beneath the surface, and it was only once she'd locked the door behind her that she was able to let them free.

Bonnie Connor was a fairly attractive woman, as attractive as any woman could be at nearly nine months pregnant. And she seemed relatively intelligent. Why would she make up such a story? Her story haunted her and she could feel the pain and agony Bonnie was suffering—if she were telling the truth. Victoria's memories of her lover's denial filled her mind, and although it hurt her deeply, she found herself mistrusting Buck more than the woman, as her sympathy leaned toward the woman so great with child. *Oh, Buck, like Armando, you've let me down. Just when I was beginning to—to love you.*

&

A rap sounded on her door at five o'clock. "Tori, are you in there? Open the door, I have to talk to you. Tori?" The rap sounded again. Louder this time.

The last thing she wanted to do at that moment was talk to Buck. "Go away."

"No, I'm not leaving until you open this door."

"Go away, Buck."

"You open this door right now or I'll break it down."

"You wouldn't dare."

"I'm going to count to three, Tori. One. Two—"

She hurried to the door, twisted the safety bolt, and flung it open wide. "All right, the door's open. What do you want?"

He pushed past her, his eyes blazing. "I want to know why you left like that. If I hadn't had a waiting room full of patients I'd have come after you. Surely you didn't believe that woman's story."

She slammed the door. "Why shouldn't I believe her? You think women go around accusing men of fathering their children without just reason?"

"She did. She's crazy," Buck shouted in his defense.

"She's desperate, Buck. Can't you see that? Men should take responsibility and face up to it instead of leading a woman on and then deserting her after—" She stopped, afraid if she said one more word, she wouldn't be able to hold back her tears any longer.

"After what?"

"After—after—oh, you know what I mean. Don't make me spell it out for you."

Buck shook his head in exasperation as he paced about the room. "I can't understand how you can take the side of a woman you don't even know."

"Because I've been there, Buck!" The words slipped out before she could stop them.

He stopped dead in his tracks. "Been where? I don't get it."

She had to figure out a way to explain her words. She couldn't let him think she'd been promiscuous. "I mean, I have a friend whose boyfriend left her when he found out she was pregnant. She–she stayed with me for awhile. I saw how miserable she was, facing her pregnancy alone."

"The rat didn't help her at all?"

She bit her lip. Lying had never been easy for her. "He denied being the father."

"The jerk."

She moved to the door. "I'd just as soon you'd leave, Buck."

He followed her but paused in the doorway. "You don't believe me, do you?"

"I–I don't know what to believe at this point. Please just go. I'd like to be left alone."

An angry look covered Buck's face as his hand grasped the doorknob. "Look, I don't have to prove myself to anyone. Not even you. Believe what you want." And he stormed out.

❧

Victoria gave Buck her two weeks' notice at the clinic. She decided she would leave Anchorage at the end of the month and return home to Kansas City, despite Jonathan's pleas that they stay. Her mother and Ron seemed quite happy, and Victoria knew her mother was in good hands. Abigale loved Alaska and, more importantly, she loved Ron. And he loved her. Their marriage was good.

Victoria kept her distance from Buck, her illusion shattered. As far as she knew, Bonnie Connor had left him alone.

Exactly one week before she was scheduled to leave, Buck invited her and Jonathan to go along with him and Micah on his monthly visit to the bush country. She refused, not wanting to be anywhere near the man. But when she saw her son's disappointment, she relented.

It was the first time she'd ridden in Buck's little seaplane and she had to admit he was a good pilot, although she white-knuckled the skinny armrest all the way.

It seemed hundreds of Indian people were there to greet them when they landed, all with smiling faces, all glad to see Dr. Silverbow.

"I could use your help," he told her as he pulled box after box from the cargo area of the little plane. "Sometimes my nurse comes along to help."

She nodded, not knowing exactly what she was getting into, but willing to lend a hand.

"We'll set all this stuff up on the little table over there by that hut," he instructed. "And bring that small metal case from behind the front seat."

Within fifteen minutes Buck was examining people, giving them the medicine he'd brought with him, administering shots to newborn babies, listening to the elderly complain about their rheumatism, and checking pregnant women. In exchange for his services, some people gave him beads, another a handmade leather belt, one a hand-carved statue of an eagle. Several others gave him animal pelts, and some gave him nothing but a toothless smile of thanks. Even Victoria received a gift—a colorful bead necklace one of the

Indian woman had woven.

"They're a proud people," he told her when they had a slight break. "I don't expect any pay. I've told them that, but they want to pay for my services even though most of them have little of this world's goods. To refuse to accept these things would insult them."

Victoria helped where she could while Micah and Jonathan played with the Indian boys. She smiled as she watched them dart between the humble dwellings. Even the language barrier didn't keep them from having fun with the Indian children.

Watching Buck amazed her. His dedication was tireless. He greeted patients as if each were most important, taking time to listen to them, encouraging them, and being their friend. *Is he living a double life? Or is Bonnie Connor falsely accusing him, and he's as honorable as he appears on the surface?*

When it was time to board the little plane and head for home, Micah and Jonathan were nowhere to be found.

"They said they was gonna go exploring," an Indian boy who looked to be about fourteen said. He pointed toward a huge mound of boulders off in the distance. "I told them they better hadn't go, but Micah said it'd be okay."

Buck looked quickly at his watch. "If we don't get out of here within the next hour, we won't make it until morning. Too dangerous to take off after dark in a seaplane."

"Normally Jonathan would have asked my permission to go off like that," she told Buck. "This isn't like him."

"Don't panic," he said calmly. But Victoria saw the concern in his eyes. He was as frightened as she was.

She bit her lip. Her heart pounded with alarm. "I'm trying not to panic, honest I am, but where could they have gone? And why aren't they back? You'd told them what time you had to leave, and both boys were wearing watches."

"Don't know, Tori. But I'm going after them. You stay here with—"

She grabbed onto his sleeve. "Oh, no you don't. I'm going with you."

"No," he said firmly, pulling from her grasp. "They may still be here in the village. I'll take some of the men with me, and you find a couple of the women to help you go door to door. They may be in one of the huts playing with some of the children."

His idea seemed best at the moment, and already women in the group were beginning to volunteer to help her.

Victoria's voice quivered. "All right, but hurry, Buck. Our boys may have lost their sense of direction and be wandering around trying to find their way back."

"And they may be right here," he assured her as he moved away, signaling several of the men to join him. "Don't worry, I'm sure they're fine."

Fine? In this strange place? Victoria watched Buck issue orders to the men, telling them to move off in different directions.

The door-to-door search yielded nothing. No one had seen the boys in over two hours. Victoria was frantic. Even though several women invited her to come into their homes, she refused. She had to stay by the little plane in case their boys came running back.

By ten, there had been no sign of the boys. The night air had become quite cool, and an older man, whom Buck had treated earlier that very day, had built a small fire at the edge of the clearing where she could warm herself as she sat on a log and waited.

I should've gone with him. She fingered the bead necklace the woman had placed about Victoria's neck and listened to the night sounds crowding in all around her. *Why do I always let a man dominate my thinking?*

Suddenly male voices pierced the eerie silence as Buck and the members of his search party stepped out of the darkness.

"Did you find them?" Victoria screamed as she ran toward

him, searching the group for the two small boys.

Buck didn't have to answer. The look on his face said it all as he shook his head sadly.

She flung herself into his arms and began to cry. "Oh, Buck. What are we going to do?"

His shoulders slumped in defeat. "Not much else we can do tonight, except keep the fire going and hope they find their way back."

After giving words of encouragement, one by one the others left for their homes, leaving the couple alone by the fire.

Her eyes widened and she began to beat upon his chest with her fists. "This is all your fault. If you hadn't insisted we come up here—"

He grabbed her wrists and held them tightly in his big hands. "Okay, Tori, blame me if it makes you feel any better. But right now it really doesn't make a whole lot of difference whose fault it is that we're here. What is important is that our boys are missing."

She quit struggling, knowing he was right. And she knew it was no more his fault than it was hers. She was the one who had said yes when he'd invited them. She could have said no. "I'm sorry. It's just that I'm so worried."

He loosened his grip and pulled her into his arms. "Me too. Micah has never done anything like this before. He's older. He should have known better."

"Is there nothing we can do?" Victoria asked with frustration as she leaned into the strength of his warm body.

"Nothing but wait for dawn. The terrain here is too dangerous to search at night."

"But the boys—"

"Remember, Tori, Micah is an Alaskan. He's hunted with me many times. Hopefully, he'll remember the things I've taught him, and he'll find a secure place for them to spend the night. He knows we'll be looking for them at dawn."

"Secure place?" she asked, her eyes damp with tears. "Out there?"

"Like between a couple of old logs or in between big rocks. He knows what to look for to keep. . ."

Again, panic set in. "Keep what?"

Buck looked as if he wished he hadn't started that sentence. "W—warm," he stammered. She knew that was not what he intended to say.

She pushed away from him. "Away from wild animals! That's what you were going to say, wasn't it?"

"Yes. I was going to say wild animals, but it isn't likely they'll meet up with any."

She knew he was trying to cover up the danger the boys might be in, for her sake. "I know they're scared, and they only had on sweaters. They'll freeze out there."

"Now, Tori," he said, his voice low and soothing, "don't worry so much. They'll probably huddle together, maybe even cover up with some pine branches. They may be asleep even now."

Her hands rubbed at her forehead. "But Jonathan is only seven. He's never—"

Buck wrapped his long arms about her and rested his bearded chin in her hair. "But Micah has. He and I have camped out many times. He knows what to do."

She relaxed a bit and leaned against Buck. Only moments before she'd felt chilled to the bone, her nerves jangled with fright. "He's all I've got," she explained as the two stood there in front of the fire, their silhouettes reflecting on the little plane parked in the middle of the clearing. "I don't know what I'd do if I lost him."

"Shh, none of that kind of talk. The men will be back at the crack of dawn and we'll find them, I promise you."

She let out a big sigh. "Don't make promises you might not be able to deliver. That's what people have been doing to me all my life."

"Well," he said in a hushed tone as he planted a kiss on her forehead, "Buck Silverbow doesn't make a practice of making promises he can't keep. You have to trust me, Tori. We'll find them."

"I'll try, Buck. But my luck with men who've made promises hasn't been too good."

He took her hand and led her to a huge log near the blazing fire. "I'm going to get the little blanket I carry in my plane. Sit here. I'll be right back."

She dropped onto the ground and wrapped her arms about her legs and watched as he walked to the plane and back, so tall, strong, and confident. Perhaps he was right. Perhaps the boys would be all right until dawn.

He sat down beside her and wrapped the blanket of red, green, and blue about both their shoulders, cocooning the two of them.

Neither felt sleepy as they stared silently into the flames of the fire. They watched it flicker and sparks spiral into the air.

"You must be frightened too, Buck. You've already lost your wife and your mother. . ." Victoria's voice trailed off. She gulped as words failed her.

"I'm not losing Micah," he said in a soft, but firm voice. "Don't even think like that."

"But it could happen. There are a dozen things that could have happened to the boys. Aren't there bears up here?"

"Sure, there are bears, but the boys probably didn't have any food with them. Or if they did, they probably ate it earlier. That's what attracts bears—food."

"How about wolves?"

"Yes, there are wolves, but they aren't interested in two little boys," he told her, as if she'd asked a foolish question.

"You're not lying to me, are you?" she asked, her eyes misty with concern. "Just to make me feel better?"

He pulled her closer. "Cold?"

"Don't change the subject."

"No, I'm not lying to you. How many stories on the news have you heard about bears or wolves attacking little boys?"

She thought about it a bit, and he was right, she hadn't heard any. But then, she lived in Kansas City. Would news stories of that sort reach all the way from Anchorage, Alaska, to Kansas City?

"There's more bears and wolves up around Denali National Park than there are near here," he assured her. Buck nestled his chin in her hair. "At least there are no snakes in Alaska."

"Do you suppose God is punishing us?"

Buck appeared thoughtful. "Could be. What makes you say that?"

"Because I deserve punishment, I guess."

"No more than I do."

"But you're a fine man, Buck. You're a good father and a great doctor. Just look at all the good you did today for these people. Other than trying to be a good mother, I'm of no value to anyone."

The tip of his finger lifted her chin. "I'd say that's about the most important job in the world, and it looks to me as if you're doing a mighty fine job of it. That Jonathan's a great kid. You should be very proud of what you've accomplished with him. And alone, to boot."

"But, you don't know the real me. I've made such a mess of my life."

"I find it hard to believe that, Tori."

"I broke my parents' hearts by deceiving them when I was in college. I dated a boy they knew was trouble, but would I listen to them? No. I sneaked around behind their backs and lied about where and with whom I was going. Just to be near him," she confessed tearfully. Her heart felt as if it would burst with worry over her son.

"You're not the first girl to do that."

"But I'd never defied my parents before. I was always that

good little girl, the one that never did anything wrong. Until I met Armando."

"Is he Jonathan's father?"

She nodded. "Yes."

"Ah, you two had to get married?"

She sat up straight. "No, it was nothing like that."

"Then how was it?"

She blinked her eyes and swallowed hard. "Guess you deserve to know the truth, now that we're related. Since you and Ron are part of our family now, it'll all come out at one time or another."

"I got plenty of time to listen." He leaned back onto the log and pulled her back with him, cradling her in his long arms.

"I'll leave out all the gory details. I'm sure you don't want to hear those."

He grinned. "Suit yourself. It's your story. Tell it any way you like."

She sucked in a deep breath and let it out slowly. "When I went off to college, my parents reminded me of the usual things. You know, the birds and bees story and how I should be careful and not get into any compromising situations; that sort of stuff. And I believed them and fully intended to take their advice. At first I only dated the guys with whom I'd gone to high school. But one night as I was walking back to my dorm, this car pulled up beside me, and I immediately recognized the man who was driving. Everyone on campus knew him. He had come to the States from Acapulco to attend college. His dad was some kind of ambassador or something, and very wealthy. Armando was the star tackle on our football team. Well, anyway, he offered me a ride, and I was so flattered by him paying attention to me, a little freshman, I accepted."

"Not a smart move, huh?"

"Things were okay then. And next, he invited me to a

movie. I really thought I was big stuff, and again I accepted. We had a great time. He was funny, attentive, and polite. When I told my folks about him, my dad immediately asked me what the man saw in me that made me special. It was a fair question, only I took it as an insult. Both Mom and Dad tried to tell me it was a little unusual for a star football player to be interested in a freshman girl, unless he was looking at her as an easy target. They told me to stay away from him."

"Wow, your dad didn't pull any punches, did he?" Buck whistled. "Bet that set up your dander."

She offered a feeble laugh. "Sure did. I stormed out of there and decided I'd date Armando and never let them know. Well, to make a long story short, we dated constantly for the next few weeks. He drove a brand new Mercedes convertible; believe me, all my friends were envious. I really thought I was something. I practically deserted my friends. Everything in my life revolved around Armando."

"I think I know where this is leading."

"I wish I'd been that perceptive." She sighed. "Well, to go on—I had visions of standing by Armando's side at his graduation, then the two of us going off to Acapulco to be married in wedded bliss the rest of our lives. I thought I'd live in a fine home— you get the picture."

"Didn't quite work out that way?"

"No, not at all. One night after we'd been to a party where Armando had had a bit too much to drink, he drove us to a deserted spot and began to kiss me. I loved his kisses, but that is as far as we'd ever gone. Even though I was in awe of him, I'd made it clear from the beginning I was a virgin and intended to stay that way until I was married."

"And he went along with it?"

She paused thoughtfully. "Yes. I thought he respected me for it. But that night, he came on strong, and I tried to tell him to stop—"

"But he wouldn't?" Buck interjected.

"No. I told him no over and over, but he was like an animal and way too strong for me. He—" She wiped her eyes. "He forced me, Buck. And he really hurt me."

Buck's fingers stroked her hair. "I'm so sorry."

She continued. "Afterward, he acted like it was all a joke and said I'd seduced him. He warned me if I said anything to anyone, he'd deny it and all his buddies would back him up on his story. They'd all say they had—" She began to cry uncontrollably.

"You don't need to say it. I get the message. What a bunch of scumbags. It's guys like them that make it hard on the rest of us. No wonder women don't trust men when they hear stories like that."

"After that night, Armando totally ignored me. It was like he didn't even know my name. And all his buddies made snide, sexy comments to me. And then I realized I was pregnant."

"And you two had to get married and then got a divorce later?"

"No. I wish that was the way it turned out. He spit in my face and called me awful names. He said he was going to go back to Acapulco to marry his high school sweetheart, and he never wanted to hear from me again. He refused to even acknowledge he might be the father of my baby. He even accused me of being with a lot of other guys. But honest, Buck, he was the only one, and it was only that one time. I wanted to die."

"Oh, you poor thing. What did your parents say?"

She twisted at the little ring on her pinkie finger. "Of course, they were devastated and Daddy said, 'I warned you.' But they stood behind me. Some of my relatives suggested abortion, but I couldn't do that. I was a real embarrassment to my parents, I know. And I was so ashamed, I could barely hold up my head."

"So, you had little Jonathan?"

She nodded. "I'd considered letting him be adopted by a couple in our church. I was so young, naïve, and certainly not equipped for motherhood. But the closer it came time for him to be born, the more I felt I would be the best one to raise him." She sighed. "Someone else might have made another choice. But that seemed to be the best way for me. It wasn't easy, though."

"Tough, huh?"

"At times."

"And he was born with that twisted foot? That must have made it even harder."

"To this day I think Jonathan's foot was God's way of punishing me." She blotted her tears on the edge of the fluffy blanket.

Buck stared into the fire. "I understand that feeling. That's the way I felt when Claudette drove our car onto the track in front of that oncoming train."

"It's not the same, Buck. You hadn't done anything to deserve that kind of punishment. I went against everything my parents had taught me, and against all the things I'd learned from the Bible since childhood."

"You didn't know me then, Tori. All I could think about was success—as a doctor, I had plans to move to Vancouver and open a large clinic, then on to Seattle to open a second one. I wanted my clinics to be on the cutting edge of medicine. I wanted the name Dr. Buck Silverbow to be a household word. I loved my family, but I rarely spent any time with them. I was too busy attending this conference and that convention, rubbing elbows with some of the great names in the field of medicine."

"I didn't know. I assumed you'd always wanted to be right where you are."

"Well, shows how much you know about me. When we were first married, I was a deacon in the church, on the board, the man everyone called when there was a need. Then I got this dream and I left it all to go after it. When Micah was born, I told myself I was building this medical empire for him, the son who would follow in my footsteps. I planned to leave him a legacy. But I left him and my wife behind, alone, while I put in endless hours at my little clinic and worked at being a big shot."

"And how did your wife feel about that?"

"She hated it. She never wanted any more than what we had right here in Anchorage. She begged me to forget my dream. But old smarty-pants me, I ignored her requests and forged ahead. I missed a lot of Micah's growing up years, years I now regret."

A frown of confusion clouded her face. "Do you regret the Bonnie Connor thing?"

His eyes narrowed as his voice boomed into the darkness and she knew immediately she'd said the wrong thing. "You mean fathering her baby? What do I have to do to make you believe me? I had nothing to do with that woman. At any time."

"Too bad we can't see the future before we make our mistakes, isn't it?" she said sadly, refusing to answer his question, still not convinced he was telling the truth.

He bristled. "Look, I don't have to prove my innocence to anyone. Not even you. I did nothing wrong. And I have to be honest with you, Tori, it makes my blood boil to think you'd even consider that I might be that baby's father."

"She'll probably insist on a paternity test," she shot back defensively. "Then what'll you do?"

He stared into the fire, its red glow reflecting the anger in his eyes. "That'd be a ridiculous move. She knows I'm not the father." His eyes suddenly riveted on her face. "Unlike some people I know."

His words hurt. She really wanted to believe him, but she couldn't shake the lump of doubt that still lingered in her heart.

"Look," he said with a sigh as he tucked the blanket closer about her neck, "for now, let's forget about Bonnie Connor. We need to focus on finding Micah and Jonathan."

"Oh, Buck, we can't lose our boys," she said with deep emotion, she, too, wanting to put their differences to rest.

"I know."

"I wish there was something we could do tonight. I can't bear the thought of them out there, alone in the dark."

Buck's hand stroked at his mustache. "I guess if we were on praying ground, we could pray."

She lowered her head, her voice barely audible. "I've tried to live as a Christian, attended church and all, but I haven't honestly prayed for years. I've been too mad at God."

"Seems we're two peas in a pod." He let out a long, low whistle. "I'd pray, but I don't think He wants to hear my prayers."

"Same here. How did I ever get so far from God?"

"You know, Tori, I remember standing at that altar when Claudette and I were married and thanking God for such a beautiful, Christian woman. I promised Him I'd take care of her and be the kind of husband she deserved. Then I broke that promise."

She allowed one finger to idly scrawl her son's name in the dirt as they sat on the ground. "And as a teenager I promised God I would serve Him as a missionary. I sure goofed on that one."

"I remember Dad telling me God is a forgiving God. All we have to do is ask. Wonder if it's really that simple?"

"That's what Mom told me when I told her about my pregnancy. She said God would forgive anything if we ask. But—"

"But what?"

"I never asked. I felt too unworthy."

"Me neither. I'd sunk too low. I knew a just God would condemn me for failing Him and my family."

Buck rose to his feet, poked the fire with a stick, and added new logs. The fire crackled and snapped. "We could try."

She stared up at him. "You mean it? Pray?"

"Guess it's worth a try."

"Do you think He'll be interested in hearing from us?"

"Got a better idea?"

She shook her head. "One of the verses I learned as a child said if we confess our sins, He is faithful and just to forgive them and to cleanse us from all unrighteousness, or something like that. I haven't confessed my sin to Him—the sin of disobedience to Him and to my parents, and the sin of dating a man I knew I should not be dating."

"And I never told Him I was sorry for turning my back on Him and being so angry with Him for taking Claudette and my mom from me."

"I think we have to do that before we can even begin to ask Him to protect our boys and safely bring them home to us."

Buck nodded. He extended a hand and pulled Victoria to her feet. "I'll start, but you have to jump in and help me if I need it. I haven't talked to God in a long time. I'm not sure if I remember how to do it."

"I think it'd be best if we knelt." Victoria smiled and she felt a certain peace.

The two knelt by the fire, wrapped in one another's arms as Buck lifted his face skyward. "Lord, this is Buck. I never did tell You how sorry I am for acting the way I did, putting everything in the world before You. Sometimes when I'm unable to sleep, I think things over. I don't know why You allowed Claudette and Mom to die, but I'm sorry for blaming You for their deaths. Folks have told me You have a plan and every right to do what You want. There's no reason You'd share that plan with me. But please, God, forgive me for being such a sinner and for turning away from You.

"And now," Buck squeezed Victoria's hand, "I'm coming to You to ask a favor. Be with my boy and with Jonathan—wherever they are. Protect them from anything that would harm them. Most of all, God, keep them from being scared. I love You, God, and I promise I'll read Your Word and talk to You more often.

"And now Tori wants to talk to You. She's a good woman, God. Please listen to her and grant her prayer. She's a great mom."

Moved by Buck's prayer, it was all Victoria could do to keep her composure as she began. "Lord, I'm such a sinner. From the time I was a small child, I've loved You and wanted to serve You—on the mission field, as a teacher, or wherever You wanted to use me. But I failed You. I turned away from You, and look where it got me. And as much as I love my son, each time I look into his precious face I see my sin staring back at me. He looks so much like his father. But I must confess, Lord, if I had to do it all over and go through all I've gone through just to have Jonathan in my life, I'd do it. Sin and all, because I love him so much." She took in a gulp of air and let it slowly escape. It helped her to keep from crying.

"You had a Son. You have to know how I feel about mine. He is the result of my sin, God. The sin I have never confessed to You. I was too proud and too ashamed. Please forgive me of my sins as You promise in Your Word.

"And now, please bring Jonathan and Micah safely back to us." She felt Buck's fingers tighten over hers once again. "And be with Buck. He's lost his wife and mother, and he needs comforting. Make Yourself real to him. To both of us. I'm not much good at praying, but I want You to know I do love You, God, even though I've acted like a spoiled brat. Thank You for listening. Amen."

"Amen," Buck echoed. He threw his arms around Victoria in a big bear hug. "I think He heard us. What do you think?"

"I know He heard us," she said with renewed confidence. "Now I guess we just have to trust that one way or another our boys are in His hands."

"I agree."

"So, now what do we do?" She surveyed the darkness around them.

"We wait until morning, which is only a few hours away."

"But the boys—"

Buck sat down against the log and motioned for her to join him. "I'll bet our boys are hunkered down somewhere wondering what we're doing. They'll be fine, Tori. We've placed them in God's hands now."

nine

The men began gathering even before dawn, carrying pick-axes, ropes, and other items that might be needed to find the boys.

"I'm going with you." Victoria rose to her feet, stretched, and ran her fingers through her hair. Her whole body ached from her sleepless night in Buck's arms, leaning against the log. She could only begin to imagine how he felt, but to look at him you could never tell he, too, had spent a sleepless night. He was a bundle of nervous energy, anxious to get started.

"No, it'd be better if you stayed here. We'll be walking on some pretty uneven terrain, and I have no idea how many miles we'll walk before we find them."

She perceived his advice to be an outright order, and she straightened her shoulders. "Oh, no you don't. You're not leaving me behind. I have as much at stake in this as you do. My son is out there too."

An understanding smile curved Buck's lips. "Okay, but stay close to me, and be careful. I wouldn't want anything happening to you. You're too important to me—and Micah."

She fell in step behind him, her eyes scanning the approaching horizon for any sign of the two children.

"Don't worry, Missy," a toothless old man told her as they moved along. "We'll find them. For Doc."

They walked for nearly two hours before stopping to rest. Victoria was exhausted, but she'd never admit it.

❧

Buck knew Tori was tired, and he wished they could linger longer, but they had to move on. He'd never let her know, but he was greatly concerned for the boys' safety. There were dangers out there she'd never even imagined. Most of the night, after confessing his sins to God and asking for forgiveness, he'd spent in silent prayer. It felt good to pray again. He'd forgotten the comfort prayer could bring.

"Here, take a drink of water." He passed his canteen to her and watched as she took large gulps.

"We'd better go on," one of the Native American men told him in a whisper.

Buck assembled the group, but before they continued the search he invited them to pray with him. Some bowed their heads, but most stared at him in disbelief, as if wondering why a man would take time for such foolishness when his boy's life was at risk.

He pulled off his hat and reached for Victoria's hand, then lifted his face heavenward. "Father God, it's me again. Once more I bring our request to You for our children's safe return to us. Wherever they are, comfort them and make them know we're coming to find them. Please, God, lead us in the right direction. And we'll praise You, I promise. Amen."

The smile on Victoria's face melted his heart as he forged ahead, her hand in his.

An hour later, Buck lifted his hand and the party came to a halt while he prayed a second time.

A little farther up the trail, they found Jonathan's backpack hanging on a tree branch. "They probably knew they were lost and left that as a sign to us they'd gone this way," Buck said excitedly as he handed the bag to Victoria, his faith renewed. "This is the first clue we've found."

She held it close and took it as a sign from God.

They continued on, slipping and sliding on the jagged rocks. One of the men took Buck aside, and although Victoria was too far away to hear their conversation, from the look on Buck's face she could tell he was worried.

"What? What did he say?" she asked as she worked her way over the rocks to his side.

"Better you don't know."

She tugged on his shirt. "Tell me this instant!"

He lifted both palms toward her. "Okay, I'll tell you, but promise me you won't get upset. Remember, we've turned our children over to God."

"I promise. Just tell me."

"He said we are heading in the direction of a deep, jagged crevice. That if it was dark when the boys reached it, they—"

She gasped and looked as though she were going to faint. Buck grabbed her and held her close. "Tori, don't. We're not even sure they came this way. They may have taken a turn where we found Jonathan's bag. God, Tori, trust in God."

His words were consoling, but inwardly, he was even more frightened than she. He'd flown over that area, he knew how treacherous it was. If the boys—Buck willed himself to forget about the what-ifs.

Finally, they reached the area above the menacing crevice, but the boys weren't there.

"We'd better turn back and go the other way," one of the men told Buck. "The boys aren't here."

"Hold on." Buck fell to one knee and bowed his head. "God, I need Your help. Give me wisdom and guidance. Show me the way to go."

"Better hurry," the man said. "Those boys are probably hungry and cold."

"Not yet," Buck told the man with a glance toward Victoria, who was standing a few yards back where he'd told her to stay. With that, he lifted his head high, put two fingers in his mouth and let out a loud shrill whistle that seemed to split the sky. And then he listened. "If Micah hears that, he'll whistle back. It's kind of our code."

Nothing.

Again, he whistled.

Again, nothing.

"Oh, Buck," Victoria cried out as her hands flew to cover

her face. "Where are they?"

One more time, Buck lifted his fingers to his mouth.

Somewhere off in the distance a faint sound echoed back, an exact repeat of the sound Buck had made.

"It's him!" Buck shouted with joy. "Tori, we've found them!"

"Which way did the sound come from?" the Native American asked as he turned his head from side to side.

"Oh, Buck, whistle again," Victoria pleaded, her face aglow with happiness that they'd located their sons.

Again, Buck whistled.

This time the sound that echoed back was a little stronger.

"Son! Where are you?" Buck hollered, his big hands cupped around his mouth.

"Down here," the answer came back faintly but clearly.

Victoria let out a loud gasp and grabbed onto one of the men for support.

"Dear God, they've fallen into the ravine," Buck exclaimed as he moved quickly toward the edge, trying to look over the side.

"Buck, be careful," she shouted, reaching toward him. "I can't lose you too!"

"Toss me a rope," he called, and one of the men quickly pulled a long coil of rope from his shoulder and threw it toward Buck. Three other men moved as close to the edge as they dared and held onto one end while Buck tied the other end about his waist.

"I'll go. You stay," a short muscular man told Buck as he cautiously climbed across the rocks and tried to take the rope from Buck's hand. "I'm used to climbing on rock. You're not."

But Buck wouldn't hear of it. It was his son who was down there.

"Ask him if he knows where Jonathan is," Victoria called out, afraid her son might be down there with Micah and possibly hurt.

"Is Jonathan with you?" Buck called out as he began his descent over the rocks at the head of the crevice.

"Yes, I'm here," came a frightened seven-year-old voice.

"Oh, are you all right?" Victoria called as loudly as she could.

"My arm hurts really bad," the child answered.

"How about you, Micah? Are you all right?" Buck yelled out as he began his descent, disappearing over the edge of the ledge as the three men held onto the rope.

"I think I broke my ankle," he answered back weakly. Everyone who heard him could hear the pain in his voice.

"Pull me up," Buck shouted from over the ledge. "Quick!"

From the look on his face as he appeared, it was obvious there was a problem.

"Rope's not long enough. They're way down there, on a ledge." He stood to his feet, giving the men a well-deserved rest from holding his weight.

"I've got a rope." The muscular man hurried forward, taking the loop of rope from his shoulder and tossed it to Buck.

Buck smiled and carefully knotted the new rope to the one that was tied about his waist. "Let's give it another shot."

"Could you see them?" Victoria asked, relieved they were alive.

"Yes, but they're a long way down there. Good thing that ledge was there or they'd be—" He stopped. "God was with them, Tori."

She smiled at him. "I know. I've been thanking Him."

A fourth man joined the others in holding the rope and Buck disappeared over the side again, this time descending hand over hand.

If only I could get near enough the edge to see them, Victoria reasoned as she warily moved forward.

"You stay there," the fifth man said firmly. "It's too dangerous."

She yielded to his command, knowing it was for her good.

It seemed an eternity before Buck surfaced again. "Any more rope?"

They all shook their heads.

"You still can't reach them?" Victoria asked as panic froze her to the spot.

"No, the rope is a good twelve feet too short." He dropped onto one of the flatter-topped rocks, his head in his hands. "Oh, God, show me what to do."

The search party stood staring at the man. No one had any suggestions. Suddenly, Buck stood to his feet and pulled his belt from his trouser loops, the belt one of the Native Americans had given him in exchange for his medical services the day before. "Anyone else have a strong leather belt?"

A taller man who had pretty much remained silent offered his. Buck fastened them together and slung the looped belts over one shoulder. "Hang on tight, men. I'm going to bring them up."

"How?" Victoria hollered as he was about to disappear over the edge.

"Just have faith in me and pray."

She breathed a frantic plea to God. If anyone could rescue the boys, she knew it would be Buck. Even if he had to lay down his life to do it.

❧

Buck reached the end of the rope, his feet dangling a good thirteen or fourteen feet over the boys. With one foot he kicked away from the rocky surface and swung himself nearly three feet to the left where he caught hold of a small tree growing out of the rock and held onto it. Once he was securely latched onto the tree, he let go of the rope.

"Dad, be careful," Micah called up to him.

Buck turned to look down at the boys who were perched on a small ledge, maybe six feet square, and beneath them lay the deep crevice yawning out at them like a hungry bear. One slip and he could drop past the ledge that held them and into that waiting vee of jagged rock. He lifted his face heavenward. "God, if I ever needed strength, it's now. Be my strength as You've promised."

Adjusting the looped belts that hung from his shoulder, Buck began to make his way down the jagged wall. He stepped on small bits of rock protruding out of the rocky surface, and his fingertips clung to other rocks.

Once, a rock holding his foot gave way and it bounced onto the ledge and ricocheted into the crevice. Buck held on with his fingertips and one foot, until he located another small rock on which to place his foot. The terrified boys covered their eyes.

"I'm okay, boys. I'm coming to get you. Don't be afraid." He tried to sound as if getting them would be an easy task, but at that point he wasn't sure his plan would work or that he would have the strength to carry it out. Unless God intervened.

At last, he reached the ledge and the arms of two little boys circled his neck and held on for dear life. "I'm gonna get you out of here, but first I want to check out each of you. That was quite a fall you had." It didn't take him long to realize his son's ankle was broken. And although Jonathan was in great pain with his arm, Buck was fairly confident it wasn't broken, just badly sprained, with much of the skin ripped off.

"Hey," he said, forcing a smile of encouragement, knowing much was going to be required of the two young boys in the next few minutes, "you're both going to be fine, but you're going to have to do exactly as I say. We'll be on top soon, and we'll get some food in those empty bellies of yours. I'll bet you're hungry."

Both boys nodded, their dirty faces streaked with tears, their clothing torn and tattered.

Buck stopped long enough to catch his breath and survey the path he must take to scale the steep cliff. Finally, he took hold of Jonathan. "Look, Jonathan, I'm going to take you up first since you're the lightest."

He slipped an arm about his son. "Micah, I promise I'll get you out of here. Just be patient and don't move until I get back down for you. I'm going to take Jonathan up, then take a minute to catch my breath, and I'll be back. Understand?"

Micah shook his head, his round eyes filled with fright.

"I love you, Micah. I don't tell you that often enough, but things are going to be different from now on. You're my special boy. Never forget it."

Buck turned to the younger boy. "Jonathan, I want you to climb on my back. I'm going to wrap these belts around your waist and mine and I want you to put your arms around my neck and hold on as tight as you can. I know your arm hurts but you have to do it. Whatever you do, don't let go."

Jonathan did as he was told, but Buck could feel the little boy's body tremble. "I know you're in pain, but this is the only way I can get us all out of here."

With the little boy strapped to his back, slowly Buck stood to his feet. He placed his hands and feet on the rocks he had selected to carry them up to the little tree protruding from the rock.

Each step was agony. The rocks looked secure, but he felt them pull away and roll down the face of the crevice. "Don't look down," he told Jonathan. "Look up. Your mom is up there waiting for us."

"I will," the young voice answered.

Finally, Buck and Jonathan reached the tree. Buck leaned out as far as he could, but he couldn't reach the end of the rope. "Hey, up there. Swing the rope a bit so I can grab hold."

The men responded immediately and on the third swing, Buck grabbed it. The top looked miles away, but one look down told him he had no choice. He had to make it.

"Here we go. Hang on," he told the child one last time and began to ascend the rope, hand over hand, pulling them both up with sheer brute strength, occasionally finding a niche or a rock where he could get a momentary footing. Finally, he reached the top and was greeted with cheers from the men and tears of joy and thankfulness from Victoria.

"Oh, Buck, you did it," she said as he made his way toward her and unstrapped her son from his back. She threw her arms around Buck's neck and smothered him with kisses. "I love you, I love you, I love you!" Then she gathered Jonathan in her arms and held him close, tears flowing down her cheeks.

"What about Micah?" she asked, finally realizing he'd left his son down on the ledge to bring up her son.

"Be careful with his arm," Buck told her. Then he added with a grin. "I'm going after Micah now."

"I'll go," the muscular man told him. "You're tired. It's too much to go again."

Buck stood proud and tall, his face scratched and bleeding from his climb. "He's my son, I'll bring him up. You men hold the ropes."

"But are you sure you have the strength to make the trip again?" Still cradling her son, Victoria knew she would never forgive herself for allowing him to bring Jonathan up first if anything happened to Micah. *Buck has already lost his wife and mother—could he survive losing Micah?* She shuddered as she considered the possibility. *Or what if neither of them makes it back to the top?*

The determined man drank water from the canteen he'd given to Victoria, slung the leather belts over his shoulder, and began his trek down the face of the steep cliff.

"He'll make it, Missy," the toothless man told her as he helped the other men hold onto the rope. "Doc's a good man, and he's as strong as an ox."

ᕮ

Buck rappelled himself as far down the crevice's evil face as he could, then slowly lowered himself to the near end of the rope. His breathing was labored; he'd expended more energy than he'd realized hauling Jonathan up on his back. Once again, he pushed off the wall with his foot and swung to the left until his hand was able to grasp the tree. He wrapped his leg over the sturdiest branch and turned loose of the rope, lingering only long enough to catch his breath before scaling the remaining distance, one scary step at a time. It became more and more difficult to find places to secure himself as rocks shifted beneath his feet.

"Dad, be careful," Micah called up to Buck.

Buck could hear the fear in Micah's voice and it chilled his heart. "I'm coming, Son. Dad's almost there." He chose to not look down, knowing the deep canyon below would only unnerve him. Finally, his foot reached the ledge, and he hurried to wrap his arms about the boy he loved more than his life. "How's the leg?"

"It's okay," Micah said, pain written all over his face, despite his smile of relief that his father was once again with him.

Buck took his knife from his pocket and slit the boy's trouser leg to the knee, revealing a nasty gash he knew required stitches. Further examination told him the ankle was fractured. He had to get Micah to the top and back to Anchorage as quickly as he could. The boy was close to shock from the break and the length of time in the cold night air. "I'll have us up to the top before you know it," he told his son with great assurance, despite his fears. He used the knife to cut the sleeve off his shirt, then wrapped it about the boy's leg. "There, that ought to help protect your leg."

"Are you sure you can carry me, Dad? I'm heavier than Jonathan."

"Sure, I'm sure. Trust me," he said with a hug around the boy's trembling shoulders. "Just give me a minute to rest and we'll be on our way."

Buck's eyes scanned the wall. Many of the rocks he had used were now gone, dislodged to the bottom of the deep crevice. If he weren't extremely cautious in his selection of strongholds, he and Micah also would be at the bottom. Buck carefully planned the route that looked best, then gently lifted his son onto his back, securing the belts around their waists. "Listen to me, Micah. What I'm about to say is very important. I know your leg hurts, but you must wrap your legs around my waist and hang on tight to my neck. And whatever you do, don't look down. Do you understand me?"

Micah nodded, his dark eyes misty.

Buck leaned against the rock wall and lifted his face. "God," he called out in a loud voice that echoed through the canyon, "You know how much I love this boy, and I can't do this in my own strength. Help me, show me the best way up. I promise I'm going to be the father You want me to be. Just give me another chance, please."

Micah cradled his head against his father's back. "Do you think God heard you?"

Buck's face brightened as all fear seemed to vanish. "I know He heard me, Micah. Let's go!"

Despite Micah's additional weight, Buck made it to the little tree with no more effort than it had taken with Jonathan. But when the men tried to swing the rope over to him, it lodged itself between two rocks.

Again, Buck lifted his face heavenward. "God, are You there? Help us. Don't abandon us now. Give me wisdom. What should I do?"

ten

"Hey, Buck, can you hear me?" He recognized the voice of the tall, quiet man.

"Yeah, I hear you."

"I'm coming down to free the rope. Can you two hang on there for a bit?"

Buck breathed a quick prayer, *Thank You, Lord.* "Sure. Come on down, but be careful."

The man slowly lowered himself on the rope until his foot reached the place where it was snagged, then looped it around his leg and gave it a jerk.

But it didn't move.

"Hang on, let me give it another try."

Buck held his breath and stared at the man as he worked to free the rope with the toe of his boot.

"Is he going to get it loose?" Micah asked, his eyes round with trepidation.

"Of course, Son," his father said with assurance, though inwardly he was a bundle of nerves.

The man kicked at the rope several times. "Hang on. I'll get it," he shouted down to the pair.

"I know you will," Buck called back to him.

"There she goes!"

"Yeeooww!" Buck shouted as the rope swung free. "Praise the Lord!" He and Micah watched as the man climbed back to the top. Then Buck grabbed the rope as it freely swung toward him. "Got it. We're coming up!"

Victoria dropped to her knees and bowed her head. *Thank You, God. Thank You he was able to free the rope. Now, please, give Buck the strength he needs to bring them both up safely.*

Complete silence took over the group on top, both those holding the rope and those watching, each knowing if Buck was able to pull both himself and his son up that rope simply by brute strength and willpower, they would be witnessing a miracle. Most of the men had been on a number of dangerous rescues, some without success, but none so treacherous and none so far down the side of such a deep crevice. And since they couldn't get close enough to the edge to see him, no one was able to tell how far down the rope he was. They only knew as long as they could feel his weight on the rope, he hadn't fallen.

Buck could feel the flesh tearing away from his hands as he laboriously pulled both his weight and that of his son up the rough surface of the rope. But what did it matter, if he was able to make it to the top? Sore hands were a small price to pay for the life of his son. "Hang on," he told Micah with great effort. "We're almost there."

Hand over hand he climbed, each thrust more difficult than the last, as he could feel his strength waning. *God, it's so far to the top. Help me,* Buck pleaded in a whisper that only God could hear.

A Scripture in Isaiah Buck had learned as a child flooded his mind, giving him the burst of strength he so desperately needed. *He giveth power to the faint; and to them that have no might he increaseth strength.* Buck shouted, "Micah, God answers prayer. Never forget it!"

He felt two small hands tighten about his neck.

Each pull brought them one step closer to safety. Finally, they reached the top and Buck was able to pull the two of them onto firm ground. The men dropped the rope and rushed to take Micah from his back as Buck staggered toward them. They'd made it! They were safe.

Buck scooped up his son, being careful with his injured leg, and carried him to Victoria who stood weeping with little Jonathan. The four stood together, their arms around one another. Buck, breathless and in agonizing pain from his ripped hands, thanked God for answered prayer.

The long walk back to the village seemed to take forever. And although Buck wanted to carry Micah himself, the men carried Micah and Jonathan all the way, leaving Buck and Victoria to walk arm in arm back to the little seaplane that would take them home.

&

It was nearly midnight before they all arrived at the hospital in Anchorage. Jonathan's arm was stitched up while X-rays were taken of Micah's ankle.

"Sorry, Son," Buck told his son as he and the emergency room doctor evaluated the results of the X-rays. "Looks like you're going to have to stay off that ankle a couple of days until the swelling goes down. Then, old buddy, we'll have to put a cast on it."

"Aw, Dad, are you sure?" Micah asked with a groan, his skinned face wearing a frown. "I've got a game Saturday."

"No more soccer for you this season," the doctor told the boy. "From what I've heard about your adventure, I'd say you're lucky to be alive."

"If it weren't for that little tree that broke their fall, who knows what would have happened to those boys." Buck shuddered at the thought.

Everyone agreed it would be best for Micah to spend the night in the hospital. The doctor on duty gave him something to make him sleep through the night, and Buck promised to be there first thing in the morning. Buck even allowed the doctor, the same doctor who stitched up Jonathan's arm, to dress and bandage his hands after a number of protests about how they were fine and needed no attention at all.

"You were a brave little man, Jonathan," Buck said as Ron drove them back to the Lodge. "You've proven you're quite mature for a seven year old. I think it's time you have your own knife, and I'm going to get you one."

"No, Buck, not a knife," Victoria protested as she slipped an arm around her son protectively. "He's much too young."

"Now, Mother, don't be such a worrywart. I'm going to teach him everything I taught Micah when I gave him his knife." He tossed a smile her way. "You can even keep it for him until you're convinced he knows how to handle it."

"Please, Mom?"

"Well, if you promise to let me keep it for you until—okay, you can have the knife, but only under my conditions," she agreed hesitantly, wishing Buck had never brought up the subject. "But the first time I find you using it without my permission—"

"I know," Jonathan broke in with a frown, "you'll take it away from me, right?"

"Right."

"You were pretty brave yourself," Buck added with a grin. "I'll even get a knife for you."

Victoria smiled. "Now why would I want a knife?"

"Oh, there are many uses for a knife."

"Name one."

"To cut up vegetables, meat, fish. That sort of stuff. You'd love one, and I'll even teach you how to use it too. All the Alaskan women use them. I've even seen your mom use one."

"Okay, but I'm not promising I'll like that funny looking thing. That's the weirdest knife I've ever seen."

"Weird? Don't knock it till you try it."

Victoria tried to tell Buck good night at the door, but he wouldn't hear of it, wanting to make sure Jonathan was tucked in for the night before leaving.

Once Jonathan was settled and asleep, Victoria and Buck lingered over Jonathan, watching the rhythmic rise and fall of his little chest. Victoria stood on tiptoe and slipped her arms around Buck's neck. "How can I ever thank you for what you did today?" Her heart was so filled with gratitude, she was barely able to utter the words. "I'm indebted to you forever."

Buck's arms circled her waist and he pulled her close. "God did it, Tori. To be real honest, that last climb—I wasn't sure we were going to make it."

She lifted misty eyes to his as her fingers stroked his cheek. "I was praying for you every second."

"Believe me, I was praying too. And you'd never guess what happened."

"Oh? What?"

A bandaged hand rose and cupped hers as it caressed his cheek. "I actually remembered a Scripture I'd learned when I was about Micah's age. Shot right through my mind as we hung there on the side of that crevice. Hadn't thought of it in years. Had to have been God made it surface to my memory when I needed it most. I think it's in Isaiah."

"Say it for me."

Buck's brow creased as he tried to remember where in Isaiah the verse was found, but it wouldn't come to him. "He giveth power to the faint; and to them that have no might he increaseth strength."

"And He did, didn't He? Increased your strength when you needed it most?"

Buck nodded, then kissed Victoria's forehead. "I knew you were praying for me. I could feel it."

His kiss trailed to her cheek, then slowly as she lifted her face toward his, he found her lips. It wasn't more than a brotherly kiss, at first. But as he looked into her eyes, it took on a different meaning, and he found himself unable to stop as his lips pressed against hers in a way they had when he had kissed his wife. Buck realized his feelings for this woman were more than that of a friend or a stepbrother.

Victoria pushed away slightly. "I—ah—we—"

But Buck pulled her to him, this time taking her into his arms and smothering her face with kisses. "Tori, I—"

Her fingers covered his lips. "Don't, Buck. Please."

"But—"

She pushed him away. "It's late, you'd better go. You promised Micah you'd be there early."

Buck didn't want to go. He wanted to stay there with her, never leave her again. Was he falling in love with this woman? Or was it only the life-threatening day they'd experienced that was bringing them together in a way they'd never known before? He didn't have answers. He only knew he wanted to be with Tori. Tonight. Tomorrow. Forever.

"Please, Buck. Go. We're both tired."

He bent and kissed the top of her hair and caught the scent of their campfire still lingering there. "Try to get a good night's sleep, and I'll check in with you tomorrow after I see my early morning patients."

"You're not going into the clinic tomorrow, are you?" she asked with surprise, knowing all he'd been through.

"Sure, why not? My patients are expecting me."

"But—your hands."

He held up the two bulky bandages with a teasing grin. "Think a few scratches are going to stop me? No way, I've got things to do."

She shook her head. "You're incorrigible. If you're going to the clinic, so am I. I'll see you there in the morning."

He frowned. "But what about Jonathan?"

"Mom will look after him, and thanks to you he's fine. That arm of his was a small price to pay for his disobedience."

"Yes, as soon as the time is right, I think our two boys had better face up to all the trouble they caused. You in agreement?"

"Absolutely. Now go on home."

Although exhausted, Victoria had a difficult time going to sleep. Buck had kissed her! And despite her vow to never let a man get that near to her again, she found herself wanting him to stay, to continue to hold her in his arms. And his kisses were different than Armando's. Buck's were tender and loving. Armando's had been rough and domineering. At times, he'd even made her lips swell from the pressure he'd put on them. Morton's kisses, on the other hand, were always dry and passionless. She'd never experienced kisses like Buck's before, and she liked them. Craved them.

Stop, you stupid woman. Haven't you learned your lesson? she asked herself in the darkness of her room as she lay staring at the ceiling. *You thought Armando was in love with you and look what happened. Sure, there're some fine men in this world, but are you smart enough to know which are the good ones and which are the bad ones? And who would want a woman like you? A woman gullible enough to allow herself to be compromised. Couldn't you see what was coming? Were you that naïve? Why would Buck be interested in you, a single mom with a young son? A woman with—what did Buck call it—baggage?*

She flipped onto her stomach and buried her face in the pillow. *Oh, God, I've been fooling myself all these years, telling myself I didn't want or need another man in my life. I do! And I want him to be a man like Buck.*

Victoria sighed. *But Buck is so in love with the wife he lost, he'd never even look at another woman. I've seen the way he stares at her picture, the loving way he talks about her. He has that woman on a pedestal, and no one will ever take her place. I've got to wake up and smell the coffee! He'd never be interested in another serious relationship. I can't let myself be hurt again.*

And then, another thought crossed her mind. A very disturbing thought. *Bonnie Connor.*

❧

Buck arrived at the clinic a few minutes after Victoria. "Micah slept all night, and the swelling in his ankle seems to have gone down a bit. In a day or two I'll be able to put a cast on it and he should be feeling better. He's not going to run any races for a while, though. He was concerned about Jonathan. How's he doing?"

"Whining a bit, but thanks to you, he's fine. Mom is spending the day with him."

"I told you not to come in—"

She shook a finger in his face. "Look at those hands, Doctor Silverbow. If you can work with those, surely I can handle a few hours in the office. Besides, Mom is spoiling Jonathan, and he loves every minute of it. He won't even miss me."

Buck and Victoria worked together until noon. "One more patient and I suggest we take a half hour for lunch. Do you want pizza? Does that sound good to you?" He reached for the doorknob to the next examining room.

But before Victoria could answer, Bonnie Connor came bursting into the clinic. Her face was flushed, and she was holding her stomach with both hands.

eleven

"I'm in labor. You have to help me!" the frantic woman screamed at Buck.

"After what you've accused me of, you expect me to help you?" Buck put his hands on his hips.

"You're the baby's father, you'd better help me." Bonnie braced herself against the doorway, her face racked with pain. "Do something! I can't stand this much longer."

Buck shot a questioning look at Victoria.

Brokenhearted by this turn of events, Victoria threw her palms in the air. She had hoped Buck would never hear from Bonnie again. "Don't look at me."

Buck looked from one woman to the other, then motioned Bonnie toward the examination room. "There's a gown on the table, get yourself into it."

He turned to Victoria who stood staring at him, confused by Bonnie's sudden appearance. "I need your help—Jean's at lunch."

She turned away. "Me? No way. Forget it, Buck!"

"Tori, I'm a doctor. I don't have a choice." His tone was pleading.

"But—"

"I always have someone with me when I examine a patient. I need you. There's no one else here."

Bonnie Connor screamed out again, apparently from another labor pain. "Get in here!" she ordered between groans.

"Tori?" Buck asked.

The young woman bit her lip. She could turn and run out the door, and Buck could do nothing to stop her.

134

"Please, Tori." His voice was kind, but anxious. "Please."

"Oh, all right!" She pushed past him and into the little cubicle where Bonnie Connor was doubled up on the side of the paper-covered examination table. Her arms were folded over her abdomen, and her white face was covered with perspiration.

Buck checked his watch, then stood waiting until the pain stopped. "Lay back. Let me check and see how far along you are."

Victoria cringed as she watched Buck pull the bandages from his mangled hands, wash them, and slip them carefully into rubber gloves. She knew he was hurting. "What should I do?"

"Let her squeeze your hand when the next pain hits. And you might put a cold rag on her forehead."

"Oh, another one is coming!" Bonnie doubled up again.

Buck turned quickly toward Victoria. "Delivery time." Buck moved quickly and assembled a few items from the wall cabinet and put them on a tray. Then he moved to the little sink and began to scrub his hands again, totally ignoring the wounds. "Scrub your hands. Use that little bottle to disinfect them. I need you to help me into my gloves and a clean gown. And put one on yourself. That baby won't wait."

Victoria did as she was told.

"There're some sterile, paper-wrapped packages of towels and blankets in that cabinet. Get several. We'll need them to wrap the baby."

Bonnie screamed again and Buck hurried to her. "Baby's coming, Bonnie. I need your help. Try to relax and—"

"Relax?" Bonnie grabbed his sleeve, her face writhing with pain. "I hurt! Can't you do something? Give me something?"

"Not if you want a healthy baby," Buck explained as calmly as he could. He stood at her feet, staring at the tip of the baby's head. "Don't push until I tell you. Have you had any Lamaze classes?"

The woman shook her head. "Don't even know what they are. Oh, I can't stand this. Do something!"

Victoria listened to Buck's every command, obeying them to the letter, afraid she might make a mistake that would hurt the baby.

The hands on the clock seemed to crawl as Buck issued orders to the woman and reported on the baby's progress. Finally, with one mighty thrust, the perfect form of a baby girl emerged.

"You've got yourself a girl," Buck told the new mother as he proudly held up the newly born infant for Bonnie to see. "And she looks perfect."

The relieved woman dropped back onto the pillow, totally spent, her breath coming in short pants, her hair wringing wet with perspiration. "Good. I couldn't take much more."

Buck placed the baby in the sterile blankets Victoria was holding and turned to her with a victorious smile. "We did it. Wrap her up and put her under that lamp. I've already turned it on. She'll be fine until I can tend to her. Right now, I need to finish up with Bonnie."

Victoria took the precious bundle in her arms, carried her to the little basket under the heat lamp, and carefully placed her there. She was feeling a euphoria she'd never experienced before.

The baby was beautiful. Her tiny pink face, her hair thick and dark. Victoria winced. Buck's hair was thick and dark. *Could he be—?*

"Victoria, I asked you to bring me another blanket. I don't want Bonnie to get chilled."

Victoria pulled her attention from the little basket and immediately went to the cabinet. She took another sterile package from the shelf, ripped it open, and covered the woman who'd just given birth to the baby Victoria feared might be Buck's. Then she stood idly by as Buck finished up with Bonnie and moved to the baby, deftly cleaning the precious child before wrapping her tightly in a fresh blanket and slipping the tiny little cap onto her head.

"Looks like Bonnie has left us. She's sound asleep. I gave her something to make her rest." He pulled the gloves from his hands and dropped them into the waste bin. "You did great. I couldn't have done it without you."

Her impulse was to slap him. The thought of a man denying his paternity made her sick. But what if he were telling the truth? Again, that old question surfaced. Why? Why would Bonnie lie about such a thing? What did she have to gain? Support money? And from a near stranger? None of it made any sense. And, after all, hadn't Buck saved Jonathan's life? Didn't she owe him the benefit of her doubts?

"She is beautiful, isn't she?" Buck whispered as he leaned over the basket and smiled at the baby he'd just delivered.

"Yes, she is," Victoria conceded as she joined him. "I'd love to have a baby girl. All I ever wanted out of life was to get married and have babies. And while I'm thankful for Jonathan, I wish I could have had a little girl too."

"Too bad she's coming into this world like this. Apparently her father doesn't want her any more than Jonathan's father wanted him." His voice was filled with sympathy and compassion.

His words brought tears to her eyes but she pushed them back. "I can't imagine a father denying his child." She gazed at the delicate infant in the funny little hat.

Buck's arm slipped around her shoulder. "Neither can I, Tori. If that baby were mine, I'd claim her in a heartbeat."

And for that one moment, she almost believed he was telling the truth.

"What do we have here?" Jean asked with raised brows as she entered the little room. "Looks like you two have been busy while I was at lunch."

Buck put his fingers to his lips and pointed to Bonnie, now strapped onto the narrow table. "Whew, am I glad to see you!" Buck whispered to the woman who'd assisted him through many births. "Take over, will you? And you'd better call the hospital and have them send over an ambulance. I don't want any complications. Not with this woman."

"Gotcha." Jean gave an understanding wink.

"Then I'm out of here. I owe my assistant some lunch."

"As if I could eat after what I've just seen," Victoria whispered. "I feel a bit lightheaded."

She felt Buck's arm circle her waist as he helped her out the door and into the outer office.

"You okay? You're not going to faint on me, are you?" he asked, genuinely concerned.

She shook her head, then leaned into him. "I hope not. I think I just need some fresh air."

The two walked to the little café across the street.

"I'll bet you didn't have breakfast this morning," Buck told her as he pushed open the door.

She shook her head. "No, I didn't. But I'm hungry now, and you were right, the fresh air helped. I'm feeling much better."

They'd barely been seated when an ambulance came down the street and stopped in front of the clinic. Two attendants pulled a gurney from the back, lowered the legs, and hurried inside. Within minutes they returned with Bonnie Connor strapped to the gurney with Buck's nurse close behind, carrying a little bundle wrapped in white.

"Hope that's the last we see of that woman," Buck said resolutely as he forked a bite of salad.

"I'm not so sure. She seemed pretty determined."

"To name me as the father of her baby? Well, let me assure you, I am not."

"What if she takes you to court?" Victoria avoided his eyes.

"Then I'll demand a paternity test. That'll end this once and for all. That woman's crazy!"

"Well, for your sake and for Micah's, I hope she leaves you alone."

Buck dropped his fork and stared at her. "You still believe her, don't you?"

"I—sort of."

"Well, do you or don't you? Be honest with me, Tori."

She lifted both palms. "Why would she make such accusations if there wasn't any truth to it? It doesn't make any sense."

He leaned against the chrome back of the chair. "You're right about one thing. It doesn't make any sense. I've tried to reason this out, but nothing about it gels. All I know is—I am not that baby's father. I don't care what Bonnie Connors says."

They finished their lunch in silence, and then Buck insisted Victoria go home and spend the rest of the day with Jonathan.

"I'm going to see the rest of my patients, then head to the hospital and spend some time with Micah."

❧

It was nearly seven o'clock before Buck pulled past the Lodge and on up the trail toward his little cabin. As he passed the home he and Claudette had shared, he felt compelled to stop and go inside. He made his way through the house, ending up in their bedroom. He sat on the side of the bed. He ran his fingers over the stitches on the beautiful burgundy and white sampler quilt. It was one of many quilts his wife had made, and Buck remembered the day she finished hand quilting it and had placed it on their bed. He smiled. "I miss you, Honey," he told her picture as he lifted it from the nightstand. "We almost lost our little boy, but I guess you know all about that."

He stood to his feet and paced about the room, the picture in his hands. "And today I delivered Bonnie Connor's baby. Can you believe the gall of that woman? Trying to name me as the father? I'd never cheat like that. You know that, don't you?"

The picture back in its place on the nightstand, he dropped back onto the bed. "I do have a confession to make." He rubbed at his forehead with a bandaged hand. "This is hard for me to say. I—I have feelings for Tori. Feelings I don't understand." He stared at the picture. "Now, don't get mad. Hear me out. I could never love another woman the way I loved you, but—I'm lonely, Claudette. And Micah needs a mother. I try, but it's just not the same."

He gulped and swallowed hard. "Tori's a single mom and she has a great kid. He and Micah are friends. You should see them together. I'm not even sure Tori would want me. But if she would, I think I'd like to spend the rest of my life with her. But I want your approval. Isn't that silly? As if you could talk to me and tell me it's okay. I've asked God's forgiveness for turning away from Him. And now I'm asking for your forgiveness, for breaking my promise. Can you forgive me?"

He lay back on the bed and closed his eyes. *God, am I being selfish? Am I betraying my wife? Am I asking too much?*

Buck didn't hear God's voice, nor did he see visions of his wife, but an overwhelming sense of peace came over him. Buck knew his prayer had been answered.

He leaped from the bed and flung open the drapes, allowing the security light in the yard to filter in. *I've been keeping this house as a shrine, making my son live in that little cabin while our home sat here unoccupied. But no more.*

He moved from room to room, snapping up shades and flinging open drapes. *As soon as I can air out this place and get the dust out of here, Micah and I are moving back.* He could hardly wait to tell his son.

And tomorrow I'm going to ask Tori out on a real date. No kids. Just the two of us. Who knows what'll happen after that?

≈

Victoria spent another sleepless night as her thoughts kept returning to Bonnie Connor and her new baby. *If a man fathered a child, would he be so intent on having a paternity test done? Or was he just saying that to throw off everyone?*

Why, oh why did Buck and his father have to come into their lives? Things were going along so well before her mother went on that cruise and met Ron.

twelve

"I've been doing a lot of thinking lately, and I've come to realize I've been pretty foolish," Buck said.

Victoria appeared puzzled. "Foolish? About what?"

"Let's just say I'm making some major changes in my life. The first one has to do with you. How about a date? Just the two of us. No kids."

"A date. You mean like—"

His smile was infectious. "Like a movie."

"Sure. I'd love it. When?"

"How about tonight?"

"Maybe stop for a soda afterward?" she gave a shy grin.

"I'll even pop for a hot fudge sundae."

They were quite busy the rest of the day, with Victoria acting as Buck's assistant in his nurse's absence. Just before four o'clock, with only two more patients to be seen, a messenger arrived with a manila envelope in his hands. He handed it to Buck and left.

"Wonder what it is?" Buck ripped it open and pulled out an official-looking paper. His face fell and a heavy frown creased his brow.

"Buck, what is it?"

He dropped onto a chair and buried his head in his hands. "Bonnie Connor's baby's birth certificate, naming me as the father."

Victoria thought she was going to be sick. She'd just begun to trust Buck and now this. She grabbed her jacket and headed for the door.

"Tori, wait. It's not true! You have to believe me."

"Give me one good reason why," she retorted as she pushed

against the heavy glass door.

"Because—because I love you!"

Her eyes turned to fire. "Is that what you told Bonnie before you got her pregnant?" The door slammed behind her.

All the way home she thought of nothing but Buck, Bonnie, and Armando. Victoria could empathize with Bonnie. Buck was treating the new mother exactly as Armando had treated her, and all the old hurts she'd worked so hard to bury had surfaced. Yes, she loved Buck. She knew that now. But life with him would be impossible. How could she be around a man who lied and evaded his responsibility? She'd loved Armando and he'd taken advantage of her love and trust. Wasn't Buck doing the same thing? Well, this time she refused to be a victim. How could she have let down her guard? She had no other choice but to get away from Buck and back to Kansas City as soon as possible.

≈

"I'm leaving, Mom. Jonathan and I are going back to Kansas City," Victoria said that night.

"But, Victoria, you and Buck were getting along so well. Ron and I had hoped the two of you would get together. Nothing would make me any happier than to have my daughter and grandson living with us here in Alaska."

"I thought we were too, but— " Victoria didn't want to be the one to tell their parents about Buck's suspected paternity. If he wanted them to know, he could be the one to tell them. "But there are complications."

The next morning, she reminded Buck that he would need to find a replacement for her. Her two weeks' notice was nearly over. "And I'm not going to work as your assistant in the meantime," she told him. "You can get one of your other employees to help you. I'll work on the files so they'll be in good shape when I leave. But keep your distance, Buck, or I'll be out of here as quick as I can move. Understood?"

He nodded. "Understood. But I'm not happy about it."

❧

Her third and final day, Buck took a call from an attorney who said he had to see him and would be right over. "I'm pretty busy," Buck told the man. "Can you make it tomorrow?"

After being told he had something of great importance to discuss with him, Buck finally agreed and told him he'd make time for him.

When the man entered the clinic, Victoria got up to leave the room, but Buck motioned for her to stay.

"I got a call from the Anchorage Police Department," the man told Buck after they shook hands. "Seems some woman deliberately ran her car into a tree and killed herself."

"So, what does that have to do with me? Was she one of my patients?"

The man pulled a pad from his pocket. "The woman's name was Bonnie Connor."

Buck dropped into a chair, his head cradled in his hands. "Oh, no. Now why'd she go and do that?"

"No one knows, but an observer said they were sure she did it deliberately."

"What about the baby?" Victoria asked with concern for the little girl she'd helped deliver.

"I understand the baby was at the sitter's house at the time of the accident. Seems Bonnie Connor left an envelope with instructions that the baby should be taken to you if anything happened to her," the man explained.

Buck jumped to his feet, his face red with frustration. "How many times do I have to tell everyone? I am not that baby's father!"

"Well, I guess that's for the court to decide," the man told him as he shoved the little pad back into his pocket. "Until then, since your name is on the birth certificate, I guess you'll have a baby to care for. The social worker will be here with the baby within the hour."

"But—" Buck moved after the man to protest.

"Sorry. That's all I know. If I hear any more, I'll let you know. Call me if you have any questions. I'll be representing the baby's rights in all of this."

Victoria watched from her place behind the desk. *If Buck weren't the father, why would the woman plan to kill herself and claim Buck as the father? What would be the purpose?*

Little was accomplished in the clinic for the next hour as everyone waited in anticipation of the baby's arrival. Sure enough, just as the man said, exactly one hour to the minute the social worker arrived with a tiny bundle in her arms. "You Dr. Silverbow?"

He nodded. "Yes, but I'm not that baby's father."

"Well, my papers say you are. Here's your baby." She thrust the child into Buck's arms, then turned to Victoria. "Here's a bag with a few things that baby will be needing—formula, diapers, the usual stuff. But only enough for a day or two. You'll have to get more."

Victoria took the bag and watched the woman turn and march out the door. Victoria was thankful that she would soon be leaving Buck Silverbow and his duplicity. She'd been deceived by this man, and this was the final straw.

She watched as Buck pulled the blanket off the baby's face. And although she knew he was upset by the baby's arrival, she respected him for not taking his wrath out on the child. His demeanor with the precious little girl was gentle, which only led her to mistrust him even more. "What are you going to do with her?" Victoria prodded, wondering how a man could care for such an infant child.

"I have no idea," he answered honestly. "Think Abigale will help me?"

"My mother? That's asking quite a bit of her, isn't it? To take care of your illegitimate child? She's already helping your dad with Micah."

His eyes were imploring. "Got a better idea? How about you?"

"Me? Isn't it pretty nervy to ask me to take care of your baby? What do you take me for, Buck? A sucker, like Bonnie?"

"Look, Tori, I need help. This baby needs help. Have you no compassion? Even if you hate me, do you want to take out your anger on this innocent baby?" He held out the infant toward her. "Look at her."

She couldn't resist the invitation and walked over to Buck. The baby was beautiful, and her arms longed to hold her. "But I'm leaving tomorrow."

"I can't run a practice, do all the legal work this mess will require, and take care of Micah all at the same time. Please stay on for a few days, until I get this settled. I need you."

Victoria could refuse Buck, but not that precious baby. "Okay, but only for a few days. No more than a week. Then I'm leaving, and you can find yourself another sitter if things aren't settled."

"Thanks, Tori," he said gratefully, his face showing signs of relief. "That's all I ask. Jean can take care of the baby until I'm ready to go home. I'd appreciate it if you'd take the minivan and go over to Barnes Department Store and buy anything the baby needs. You can charge it to my account. Dad will unload it for you when you get back to the Lodge, and I'll meet you there later."

"Anything the baby needs? Do you have any idea how many things that will be? And what it will cost you?"

Buck pulled his credit card from his wallet. "Anything she needs."

❧

The next few days were some of the happiest Victoria had ever spent as she set up a nursery in her room and cared for the dark-eyed, pink-cheeked angel. The feeding, bathing, dressing, and rocking were all tasks Victoria enjoyed.

"This baby needs a name," she told Buck as he walked the room with the baby in his arms.

"Name? I guess you're right. You choose."

She pondered the thought. "How about Rachel? Or Serena?"

"Um, no, she doesn't seem like either of those names."

"You have a better idea? After all you are the—"

He shot Victoria a daggered look. "I am not the father."

"Touché! That hasn't been proven yet. So what are you going to call her? She needs a name. We can't just keep calling her Bonnie's baby."

Buck placed a finger under the baby's delicate little chin. "A little angel like this deserves an angelic name. How about Angela?"

Victoria nodded. "Or how about Angelica?"

"Perfect." Buck smiled as the baby grasped his finger. "See, she likes it. Angelica it is."

"Well, it's been three days since we brought Angelica to the Lodge, and it seems you're no closer to a solution than you were the day she came to stay with you. I think you'd better start looking for another baby-sitter. I'm going home at the end of the week."

"But I need you—"

Victoria backed away. "Sorry. As much as I love caring for little Angelica, I have to move forward with my own life."

"You're really going through with this?"

She nodded.

"If you insist on leaving, would you at least find a sitter for me? I'm still looking for your replacement at the clinic." He handed the baby to her. "You do want to make sure I hire a good one, don't you?"

She thought over his words. He was right: She was concerned about who would take over her jobs when she left. "Okay. But I'm leaving at the end of the week, baby-sitter or no baby-sitter. I'll get on it first thing tomorrow."

The ad she placed in the paper yielded nothing but a bunch of women she wouldn't trust with a Barbie doll, let alone a flesh-and-blood baby. And the sitters the service sent over were no better.

"What is Buck going to do with the baby when you leave?" Victoria's mother asked when the last applicant left.

"I have no idea, but I warned him. I told him I was leaving, baby-sitter or no baby-sitter, and I meant it."

"I guess I could take care of Angelica until Buck finds someone," Abigale said, but Victoria could tell her newlywed mother did not want to offer.

"No, I've already told Buck that was not an option."

The day of Victoria's departure arrived. "Well, I'm off," she told Buck as she wrapped little Angelica in her blanket, "and here is your baby."

"I don't want you to leave. I hope you know that." Buck tried to slip his free arm around her waist.

"Because you need a baby-sitter?" Victoria asked him sarcastically.

"No, it has nothing to do with the baby. I love you, Tori. I think I've loved you since the day I met you when we were both waiting for our parents to get off that cruise ship. I was too stubborn to let go of my past life with Claudette."

She breathed a sigh of resignation. "Well, it's too late now. I've loved you too, Buck, but we could never build a life on deceit. I tried that once before and I couldn't take it again. The pain is too severe and it never goes away."

"You have to believe me, I love you—"

She backed away. "That's exactly what Armando told me. Then he took advantage of me and deserted me."

"I'd never do that, Tori."

"You already have, Buck. Not to me. Bonnie Connor. She needed you and you deserted her. She faced her pregnancy alone, just as I did. I could never forgive a man who does that to a woman." She turned away, afraid she might weaken and be tempted to stay if she looked into his eyes one more time.

"I have to get to the airport. Your father's taking us. Thanks for everything, and thanks for nothing. It's been swell." And Victoria walked out of Buck's life, her heart bursting.

thirteen

A disillusioned young woman and her son arrived in Kansas City unannounced and without fanfare. The last thing she wanted was a pity party from her relatives.

Victoria threw herself into her work, the research job she'd had with her brother before leaving for Alaska. Jonathan, happy to be back with his former classmates but missing his new friend Micah, started school. Victoria was comfortable living in her mother's house. She and Jonathan quickly fell into their old routines.

"You okay?" Jason asked as Victoria placed a pile of case studies on his desk. "You've been pretty low since you got home. Anything wrong?"

She shook her head and dabbed at her nose with her hanky. "I'm fine, just coming down with a cold, I think."

He gave her a skeptical look. "Couldn't be missing that Alaskan stepbrother of yours, could you?"

"Of course not. Why would you say such a thing?"

Jason jabbed at her arm. "I kind of thought you two had something going there."

"For your information," she said briskly, "I'm considering marrying Morton. He's asked me again and I just might accept."

"What's he think about you opening your shop?"

She shrugged. "He wants me to wait until after the wedding."

"I wouldn't hold my breath on that one. I doubt you'll ever see that shop if he has his way about it," Jason said with a snort. "What's Jonathan think about having old Morton as a stepfather?"

Victoria picked up a book and thumbed idly through the

pages. "You know he doesn't like him, but he'll come around. Morton is a fine man."

"A fine, arrogant man, if you ask me," Jason retorted.

"That's your opinion." She slammed the book on the desk. "Yours and Buck's."

"Take your time making a decision like that, Sis. Till death do us part is a long, long time."

I have to forget about Buck, she told herself as she walked into her office. *I could never give myself wholly to a man who denies his child. Even if he wanted me, which I'm sure he doesn't, I could never let him touch me or make love to me. Oh, Buck, how could you? I loved you and you let me down.*

One week later on a Saturday morning, the doorbell rang just as Victoria was ready to go to the grocery store for milk. Hoping to get rid of her caller, she grabbed her purse and hurried to the door.

There stood Buck, holding little Angelica in his arms. "She wanted to come and see you." Buck smiled an easygoing grin, the one that always made Victoria's heart skip a beat.

She flung the door open wide and eagerly took the baby from him. "She can speak already?" Victoria smiled and motioned Buck toward the sofa.

"We've learned to communicate," Buck said.

"Is she wet?" Victoria sat next to Buck. She tugged the blanket from the baby's legs.

Buck laughed and pulled a disposable diaper from the bag he'd had slung over his shoulder. "Is she ever not wet?"

"I can't believe how she's grown," Victoria said, lifting the baby's plump bottom and removing the wet diaper. "Look at those chubby little legs. You must be feeding her well."

"Any credit for her well-being goes to your mom. I tried to find a baby-sitter, but she didn't like any of them and finally decided to take on the job herself. She's quite a lady."

Victoria returned his smile. "That she is. I'm not surprised she stepped in. She's never let me down, not once." She paused. "Except when we didn't get to open our shop."

"And I let you down?"

Victoria ignored his question as she tended to Angelica.

"I've been miserable without you, Tori." Buck slipped his arm around her shoulders, but she pretended to not notice.

"And one night, after you left, I was reading my Bible and came across a Scripture I'd memorized after Micah was born. Actually, it's in the book of Micah, in the seventh chapter. I claimed that verse as my own that night. It said, 'Therefore, I will look unto the LORD; I will wait for the God of my salvation: my God will hear me.' "

Victoria remembered how she learned that verse as a child. She thought of the many times her father had reminded her that even if God didn't seem to answer her prayers, He always heard them.

"I love you. I've looked to God and asked Him over and over to give me some way to show you and to prove to you, once and for all, I am not Angelica's father."

With a victorious grin he pulled an envelope from his pocket and waved it at her. "And, in His time, He provided that way."

Her eyes scanned the innocuous envelope. "That's your proof?"

"Yes, open it. And notice the seal has not been broken. I wanted you to be the first one to take a look at it." He offered it to her.

She held back. "Why do you want me to see it before you? I don't understand."

"It contains the results of the paternity test I decided to have taken. To prove my innocence once and for all."

She pursed her lips. "But what if it says you are—"

"It won't. Because I'm not Angelica's father. I've told everyone that from the beginning. There is no way I could be." His voice was filled with confidence. "Open it, please."

Slowly she took the envelope from his hand, examined the

seal, then forced open the flap. But as she reached inside, she was reminded of a Scripture she'd read that morning. *Trust in the LORD with all thine heart; and lean not unto thine own understanding.* Her understanding had led to nothing but confusion.

"Look, Tori. I know I hurt you, but I didn't do it intentionally. After all you'd been through with Armando, it's easy to understand why you'd believe the worst about me—especially when there was so much evidence against me. I'm not mad at you for mistrusting me. I love you. I want to spend the rest of my life loving you and taking care of you. I'd never willingly hurt you in any way. You should know that. Now, go ahead, open it. Please."

She fingered the brown envelope, each of Buck's words replaying in her mind, torn between truth and trust. "No, Buck. I have to tell you some things first. Hear me out, please." She bit her lower lip and let out a long, slow sigh. "All my life I've prayed if ever another man came into my life, he'd be a man after God's own heart. You've turned back to God and have promised to make Him the center of your life. And I've wanted that man to love my son and be the father Jonathan's never had. In so many ways you've shown your love for Jonathan, and you have even put your own life at risk to save his. Most of all, I've wanted that man to love me more than himself. Buck, you've proven your love for me time and time again."

Buck placed his hand on her shoulder. "I can see why you'd doubt me. That woman's—"

"Don't make excuses for me." She pushed his hand away, struggling to hold back tears of regret that ached for release. "I've denied your love by allowing little seeds of doubt to grow into straggling vines of distrust. I know I've hurt you. I've seen it in your eyes. I've heard it in your voice. I'm so afraid you'll never be able to forgive me for even considering you could have fathered that baby."

"Tori, it's okay. There's nothing to forgive." Again he tried to comfort her, but she pushed him away.

"I've held something back from you, Buck. Something I should have told you a long time ago, when I told you about Armando."

Buck smiled. He held Victoria's hand and began to stroke it with the pad of his thumb. "It can't be very important. You've told me all about that skunk. What could be any worse than that?"

"You may not feel the same about me when you hear what I have to say." She paused, biting her lower lip until it almost bled. "I—ah—because of my difficult pregnancy with Jonathan, I—"

He looked at her expectantly. "Yes?"

"I know you want a house full of children, and I—the doctor said I can't have any more." She turned away, sure this would put an end to any relationship they might have had.

"Is that all?" Buck snickered. "Sweetie, this world is filled with children who need good homes."

Finally, Victoria handed the unopened envelope to him. "Here."

"You're not going to open it? You hate me that much?"

"No, Buck. I love you *that* much. I no longer need a paternity test to prove your innocence. I know you. You'd never do such a thing. I should have realized it long ago. But old wounds don't heal quickly." She began to weep. "Can you ever forgive me for doubting you?"

He wiped her tears with his thumb. "Nothing to forgive." He pulled her to his shoulder and kissed her while the baby snuggled between them.

Victoria pulled away suddenly and stared into his eyes. "But what about the baby? Since that paper will say you're not the father, what will happen to Angelica?"

He touched the tip of the baby's round little nose, and she wiggled ever so slightly. "I thought about that all the way here, and I've come up with two choices. One, I can show these results to the court, proving I'm not her father. She will become a ward of the court and probably be sent to a foster home until she can be adopted."

Victoria shuddered at the thought. "Little Angelica in a foster home? Adopted by strangers? What's the second choice?"

"Or we can tear up the paper and let the world think I'm her father, and we can keep her as our own. That is, if you'll consent to marry me and accept another woman's child as your own."

She beamed as she considered his words. "Marry you? Oh, Buck, I never expected to hear those words. Yes, I'll marry you." She bent and kissed the sleeping baby. "And of course I'll accept Angelica as my own. Micah, too. I love you, Buck."

Buck shifted the sleeping baby into the crook of his other arm and reached into his shirt pocket. "I just happen to have an engagement ring with me—hoping you'd say yes."

Victoria found herself breathless as he slipped the ring on her finger.

"This means you're mine, you know," he said, love filling his eyes.

She lifted her hand and gazed at the sparkling diamond. "I know. Marriage is a sacred thing, Buck. God's Word is very explicit about that. This is a lifetime commitment. Are you sure you're ready for it?"

"Ready for it? How about eloping right now?"

She leaned into him and laughed. "And deprive all of our family members from seeing us tie the knot? They'd never forgive us."

He rested his chin in her hair. "You name the day."

❧

Two weeks later, Victoria stood before the mirror in the church's dressing room and adjusted her veil. In a few minutes she would become Mrs. Buck Silverbow.

"You make a beautiful bride," Abigale said to her only

daughter. Abigale held little Angelica who was dressed in an adorable pink gown. A tiny pink bow was tucked in her thick black hair.

The young woman in the white satin gown stared at her reflection. "Oh, Mom, is that happy woman really me? Am I dreaming? Am I actually going to marry this wonderful, caring man?"

Abigale grinned. "I don't want to say I told you so, but I knew Buck was the right man for you the day you told me you were staying in Alaska until you were sure I'd be happy married to Ron. You may not have realized it at the time, but I did. You wanted to stay not only for me, but you didn't want to leave Buck."

"You really knew it?"

Her mother smiled as she adjusted little Angelica in her arms. "So did Ron. We tried to make sure the two of you spent plenty of time together. Without being too obvious, of course."

A knock sounded at the door. "Tori? Let me in." It was Buck.

"No!" she said firmly. "It's bad luck for the groom to see—"

"This is important, Tori. I think you'd better let me in."

fourteen

Victoria opened the door a crack and peeked through. There was Buck, looking dashing in his black tuxedo, standing with a woman she didn't recognize. From the look on his face, Victoria knew something was wrong. "Give me a second, I'll slip out of my gown and into a dress."

He nodded. "Hurry."

Less than two minutes later, she was standing beside him, her heart pounding.

"This lady is a friend of Bonnie Connor. She says she has a message for me from Bonnie. As my wife, I wanted you to hear whatever she has to say."

"I went to Dr. Silverbow's office to deliver this letter. Before Bonnie died, she asked me to make sure he got it by the baby's third-month birthday. His nurse thought I should deliver it to him here, before the wedding," she told Victoria. The woman handed the letter to Buck. "The nurse even arranged an airline ticket for me and gave me some money. I told her it was too expensive to send me all the way to Kansas City, but she insisted."

The woman turned to Buck. "She said you'd want me to come. I'm sorry I wasn't here earlier, but I missed plane connections in Seattle."

Buck took the letter from her. "She was right, I'm sure whatever is in that letter is important. Maybe it'll answer some of my questions." He slipped a finger under the flap and ripped open the envelope. He unfolded a letter penned in a woman's scrawling handwriting and began to read.

Dear Dr. Silverbow,
First of all, I have to apologize for all the trouble I've

*caused you. I hope when you hear why I had to do it,
you will understand and forgive me. Perhaps you've
learned to love my baby after living with her these past
few weeks. I hope so. Loving her will make it easier to
hear what I have to tell you.*

Buck smiled at Victoria, knowing they already loved little
Angelica. He continued reading:

*Rocky, the baby's real father, is in prison for killing a
security guard during an armed robbery and may be facing death row. He hasn't told anyone yet, but I was his
partner. I helped plan it and drove the escape car. A friend
of his has already told me Rocky is threatening to impli-
cate me because I haven't come to see him. But I've been
too scared. I know it's only a matter of time before I'm
arrested since the police have already questioned me.*

*Even Rocky doesn't know he's the baby's father. I told
him I was raped by a stranger. I knew if the police ever
found out Rocky was the father, I would be caught. So I
had to make sure another man was named. I've spent
eight years of my life in prison, and I can't face going
back. I don't want my child to be a ward of the court and
raised by a long line of foster parents like I was.*

*I decided the best thing I could do for my baby was to
find a fine, upstanding man and name him as the father.
And you were so good to me when you treated me last
year. You probably don't remember, but your son was in
the office that day. I watched the loving way you were
with him, and I knew you'd be good to my baby.*

Buck blinked several times, then continued:

*I'm sorry for causing those scenes in your office, but
I knew I had to take drastic measures; otherwise you'd*

*never be interested in taking the baby of a woman you
barely knew. I hope I didn't ruin your reputation. That's
the last thing I wanted to do. But I was desperate. All I
could think about was my baby's future.*

*As soon as I leave my friend's house, I'm going to
take the baby to her baby-sitter, then I'm going to drive
my car into a tree. I already have the one picked out. I'll
drive fast enough that I'll be sure to die. I want to go
quick. It's my only way to escape prison.*

*Please, Dr. Silverbow, keep my baby. Your name is
already on the birth certificate. As far as the law is concerned, she's already yours. That's the way I planned it.
And if you have it in your heart to raise her as your
own, I have one more favor to ask. Never let her know
her father and mother were involved in that robbery, or
that we both have prison records. She's so sweet and
innocent. She doesn't deserve this.*

*I wish there were something I could do to make up for
all the trouble I've caused, and in some ways I guess I
am. I'm giving you the most precious thing I've ever had
in my life—my baby.*

> *Thank you,*
> *Bonnie Connor*

Buck wiped his eyes with the back of his hand. "That poor
woman. If I had only known—"

Victoria leaned into Buck and buried her head in his chest.
"Jus–just think what she went through, living a l–lie, going
through her pr–pregnancy all alone, planning her d–death,"
she said between heaving sobs.

"What's going on out here?" Abigale asked, still holding
little Angelica.

Buck rushed to take the sleeping baby and cradled her
close to him. "We'll tell you all about it later."

"Have you two been crying?" she asked as she looked

from Buck to Victoria, then to the stranger.

Victoria smiled through her tears. "She brought good news, Mom. At least part of it is good. We now know the whole story behind Bonnie Connor's strange actions. I'll tell you all about it later." She touched Angelica's little chin, then stood on tiptoe and planted a kiss on Buck's cheek. "But right now I have to get ready for my wedding."

Minutes later Buck Silverbow, accompanied by his bride and two little boys dressed in black tuxedos, stood at the altar holding a sleeping baby girl.

After the traditional wedding music, the pastor gave a Biblical challenge to Victoria and Buck. Then the pastor told the audience, "Buck and Victoria have chosen to say their own vows. Buck."

The big man shifted Angelica to the crook of his other arm and took Victoria's hand in his. He looked into Victoria's eyes. "Tori, I take you as my wife, to love and cherish for the rest of our lives. I promise I'll be the husband you deserve. I'll be faithful, and I'll take care of you through sickness and in health. And I promise to be the best father I can be to your son Jonathan, who is now my son. To my son Micah, who is now your son. And to our baby, little Angelica. I make these vows in God's presence, and I thank Him for bringing us together. Together, we'll make Him the head of our home. I love you, Tori, and I'm going to spend the rest of my life proving it to you. Thank you for becoming Mrs. Buck Silverbow."

Victoria found it hard to speak after hearing Buck's words. She forgot all the words she had practiced. She felt Buck's fingers squeeze hers and that made it a little easier. She looked up into Buck's eyes. "Oh, Buck, how can I ever tell you how much I love you? How can I put into words the joy of being with you? Just knowing you has changed my life. I promise to be the wife you deserve. Although I know I can never be the wife you lost, I promise to try to be the best wife I can be. I'm so proud Micah wants to accept me as his mother, and that you want to be a father to my son. Together, we'll raise Angelica. I'll take care of you in sickness and in health. And I'll be faithful to you."

She swallowed at the lump in her throat. "Oh, what else can I say, except I love you with my whole heart?"

Buck turned to the pastor. "May I say something else?"

He smiled and shrugged his shoulders. "It's your wedding, you can say anything you like."

"I just want to add that because of all Victoria and I have been through, we've turned back to God. He's going to be the center of our home, and with His help we'll do our best to raise our children according to His Word. Because without Him and answered prayer, we might not be standing at this altar right now."

"You may place the ring on your bride's finger," the pastor said.

Micah stepped forward and handed the ring to his father. Buck slipped it onto Victoria's hand. "This ring is a token of our love. Wear it always, my love."

Jonathan handed a gold band to his mother, and with a trembling hand she slipped it onto the third finger of Buck's left hand. "Wear it always, my love."

Buck reached into his pocket and pulled out two small gold rings and handed them to Victoria. "These are for Micah and Jonathan. We're going to be a family now and these are to remind you boys we'll always love you. Each of you is as special to us as the other. And as soon as Angelica is old enough to wear one, we have a ring for her too."

Victoria placed the rings on the fingers of two beaming boys, kissing each one on the cheek.

"I now pronounce you husband and wife. You may kiss the bride."

Slowly, Buck lifted Tori's veil, his eyes never leaving hers. He could see love reflected, love that would last a lifetime. His lips pressed hers, and he knew in his heart that Claudette was in heaven smiling her approval. He was finally at peace. Their lips parted. "I love you, Tori," he said.

The couple turned to face the many well-wishers assembled to sanction their wedding. The pastor said proudly, "I'd like to introduce you to Mr. and Mrs. Buck Silverbow and their family."

And the audience applauded.

෭

After the long flight to Alaska, Victoria and Buck and the children were tired. Once the children were all tucked in bed in the Lodge, the newlyweds sat alone in the tiny living room of Buck's cabin. He took Victoria's hand and pulled her toward the door. "Leave your jacket on and come with me. I've got a wedding present for you."

"Really? What is it? Tell me."

His eyes sparkled with mischief, but he didn't head for their little bedroom as she had supposed he would. Instead, he led her outdoors and down to the clearing where he had been carving the ugly totem pole.

"My present is here?" Victoria asked in surprise.

Buck flipped the switch on the big yard light, and there, standing alone, was the most beautifully carved pole Victoria had ever seen. "Oh, Buck. I love it." She moved to examine the magnificently carved pole more closely. "But where are the others, the ones with the grotesque faces?"

"Gone. I took them all down." He strode up behind her and slipped his arms around her waist. "They represented everything ugly in my life. They no longer belong here, not since I met you."

Her eyes scanned the tall pole from its tip to its base. "I've never seen anything like it, all those delicate flowers and vines. Where did it come from?"

"I carved it for you while you were in Kansas City." He paused. "Well, I had a little help from my carver friends, but I designed it." He pointed to the top. "See what it says?"

She took a few steps backward, where she could see it better, and read aloud: *To Tori, with love.* Her hands flew to cover her face as she began to cry.

Buck's face grew grim. "You don't like it?"

She brushed aside her tears as she ran into his arms. "Oh, Buck, I love it. It's the sweetest thing anyone has ever done for me."

"If ever you doubt my love, look to the pole, Tori. It will stand here as a constant reminder to you. I'm sure, like any other married couple, there will be times when we won't agree, but my love for you will never waver."

"How could I ever doubt your love? Your love and God's love have changed my life."

"I wanted you to see it on our wedding day." He flipped off the light and they walked arm in arm back to the cabin. "And another thing, I'm going to build us a new home. One that will be all ours, yours and mine, with no ghosts in it."

She stopped and stared at him. "I don't need a new house. The cabin is fine."

He let out a robust laugh. "For me and Micah maybe. But for five of us? I don't think so. Give me till spring and—"

Her face filled with concern. "But what about the beautiful home you and Claudette shared? You can't sell it. It's filled with too many memories."

He kissed the tip of her nose. "I'm going to save it for Micah. Someday he'll get married, maybe eventually take over my practice. I'd like for him to have it. Nothing would please me more."

"You think of everything," she said as she slipped her hand into the crook of his arm and they began the walk back to the cabin.

He bent and kissed the top of her head. "And right now I'm thinking of the love we're going to share tonight."

She wanted Buck to make love to her. More than anything else, Victoria wanted to become one with him, the husband she had vowed to love until death parted them. But old memories died hard and suddenly all she could think about was the last time a man touched her in that way. Armando. She shuddered.

"Don't worry, Tori. I'll be gentle. There's no rush. We have a lifetime."

And with his tender words, she knew the memories of Armando and the fear she'd felt all these years since that horrible night were now behind her, never to haunt her again.

As she gazed at the handsome man beside her, she knew that this night was going to be the most special night of her life.

epilogue

six years later

"How was school today?" Victoria asked the dark-haired child who stood at the table dipping her mother's famous peanut butter cookies into a glass of milk.

"Wish I was in first grade," Micah said. He groaned as he poured himself a tall glass of cold milk. "All Angelica has to do all day is play with blocks or listen to stories. I have to study history, grammar, and other dumb stuff." He grabbed one of his sister's cookies, broke it in half, and stuffed it into his mouth. "Who cares who was president during the Civil War?"

The little girl yanked her plate away and made a face at her brother. "Mom, he took my cookie."

Victoria playfully shook a finger at the boy. "Micah, there's plenty in the cookie jar. Leave your little sister alone."

"At least you get to play on the soccer team." Jonathan flipped Micah's cap from his head. "Just wait until next year. One more operation and the doctor said I could play on the team. Then I'll show you how to kick a ball."

"You'd be better off butting it with your big head," Micah teased. He picked his cap off the floor, tossed it onto a kitchen chair, and headed for the cookie jar.

"Okay, you boys stop that. Your dad will be home any minute. You don't want to ruin our anniversary with all that squabbling, do you?"

"Yeah, it's Mama and Daddy's versery. You'd better be good," Angelica warned her brothers. She took another bite of cookie.

"Hey, what's going on here?" Buck sniffed the air as he came into the room, hugging each child. "Mmm, is that peanut butter cookies I smell? Looks like Mom's been busy in the kitchen today."

"Happy versery," Angelica said and shoved a big piece of milk-soaked cookie into her father's mouth.

Buck finished chewing. "Thanks, I love your mama's cookies." He pulled Victoria away from her place at the sink where she was washing cookie sheets and wrapped her in his arms. "Six glorious years I've had with your mama. And she still says she loves me."

Victoria reached a damp hand to cup his chin. "And I love you more each day, Dr. Silverbow."

Buck squeezed her hand, then knelt to pick up their daughter. "You kids are gonna spend the night with your grandparents. Your mama and I are going out on the town to celebrate. God has given us six years together and—"

"Why can't we go with you?" the little girl asked as she twined sticky fingers through her father's hair.

"Yeah, take her with you," Jonathan said. He grinned at his brother. "She always messes up our video games."

"Do not!" Angelica retorted, her chin sticking out defiantly.

"Do so," both boys accused in unison.

Buck held up a hand. "No more of this. You boys need to be nice to your little sister." A horn sounded. "Now get your things. Grandpa Ron is waiting."

The children ran through the house and out the door.

Buck dropped into a kitchen chair and folded his hands. "Just you and me, Babe."

"Yeah, quiet around here now, isn't it?" Victoria sat down on his lap and gazed into his dark eyes as her arms slipped around his neck. "Think you can take another six years of being married to me?"

"How about eternity?" He rubbed his forehead against hers. "I wish I was a poet or a writer. I have a difficult time expressing myself sometimes. I'd like to present you with flowery words, words that would adequately describe my love for you."

She kissed the tip of his nose. "You tell me everyday with your gentleness, your loving ways. You're my hero, Buck."

He grinned. "Hero, huh? That sounds pretty good to me."

"I have an anniversary present for you," she said. With an eager smile, she stood, pulled a large flat package from behind the pantry door, and placed it on his lap. "Open it."

Buck popped the string with his pocketknife and pulled off the colorful paper. "Tori, I love it." He held up the beautiful oil painting of himself, Victoria, and the three children. "You did this from the snapshot Dad took last summer at Earthquake Park?"

Victoria nodded with a look of satisfaction. He liked her gift. She smiled. "I guess I haven't lost my touch." She leaned over his shoulder and admired the family portrait she had worked on for months.

Buck's fingers moved over the uneven surface appreciatively, touching each likeness. "I don't see how you do this. The kids look just like themselves."

"You really think so?"

"Sure do. Just look at Angelica's little button-nose. The likeness is uncanny. You are one talented lady. Too bad you have to waste that talent staying home and taking care of us. You should be doing commission work, or have your own studio." He braced the painting against the wall and took her hand and pulled her into his lap again. "Sorry you haven't had much time to paint—with the kids and all. But now that Angelica's in school all day—"

"I love to paint, Buck, but I wouldn't exchange one minute I've had with the four of you." She snickered. "I didn't even mind the dirty diapers. And besides, the art classes I've been teaching part-time at the college have helped keep me in practice."

Buck smiled, as if he knew something she didn't. "I have a present for you too. But you'll have to come with me to see it."

She nudged him. "Another beautiful totem pole?"

"You'll have to wait and see. Go get your coat."

Victoria was puzzled as the car headed toward downtown. "Is it bigger than a bread box?" she asked and scooted closer to him. "That's what my mother used to ask us on her birthday."

"Yes, I'd say so. Quite a bit bigger."

"Is it a new bread machine? The one we got as a wedding gift is getting pretty sluggish."

He frowned, but kept his eyes straight ahead on the road. "Now, would I get you a bread machine for an anniversary gift? What kind of a husband would do that?"

She poked him in the ribs. "The kind that likes fresh, home-made bread."

"I can promise you it is not a bread machine." He pulled the minivan onto Fourth Street and parked along the curb. He took a small gift-wrapped box from his jacket pocket and handed it to her. "Here."

"This is it? You said it was bigger than a bread box!"

"Part of it is. Open it," he instructed her with a look of anticipation.

"Here? Now?"

He nodded.

"But why here? Why not at home?"

"Tori, open it."

She carefully untied the ribbon and placed it in her lap.

"You're not going to keep that ribbon and use it again, are you?" Buck asked.

"I'm going to put it in our scrapbook." She gently pulled the paper off, folded it, and slipped it beneath the pink satin ribbon.

"You'd better hurry or we'll be celebrating our seventh anniversary by the time we eat and get home," he teased. "Want me to help?"

"I can do it by myself." She smiled back at him. She removed the lid and found a single brass key inside. "A key?" she asked.

"You don't like keys?"

"I don't make a habit of collecting them." Victoria spun the little key in her fingers.

"Look in the bottom of the box."

She lifted the lid again. Folded in the bottom beneath the tiny layer of tissue paper was a photograph of a building. She recognized it immediately. "This is that building over there!" She pointed her finger to a large two-story building across the street from where Buck had parked the car. "The old Wilson building."

"It's not the old Wilson building anymore. It's Tori's building. I leased it for you, for that art and gift shop you've always dreamed about opening—the dream you had to put aside when you agreed to marry me. Now that Angelica's in school all day, there's nothing to stop you."

"But how—"

He pulled her close. "I've already contacted an architect, and I have a construction crew lined up waiting to remodel it any way you want. Happy sixth anniversary, Darling."

Tears trickled down her cheeks. "I'll bet you think I'm a crybaby. It seems since I met you I've done nothing but cry."

He nestled her head against him. "You're *my* crybaby. And besides, we've been through a lot these past few years."

"Oh, Buck, this is the most wonderful present you could give me. My very own shop." She sat up and stared at the building that would soon house her dream. "What shall I call it?"

"I've been giving that some thought. I have a suggestion, but it's your shop. You can call it anything you wish."

She brushed a lock of shiny black hair from his brow. "And what do *you* think I should call it?"

"You really want to know?"

She nodded.

He took a deep breath and exhaled slowly. "I think my suggestion for a name would be appropriate under the circumstances."

"What circumstances?"

"That once you had a chance to see Alaska, you came to love it almost as much as I do."

"That's true. So what name would you suggest?"

"How about—"

Her eyes sparkled. "Yes?"

"How about—" Again he paused, enjoying this game he was playing with her.

"Buck, say it!"

"Tori's Northern Exposure Art and Gift Shop."

She repeated the words several times, then planted a kiss on his lips. "It's the perfect name." She looked again at the building. "I love it."

Buck grinned. His dream had come true too. "Remember what I told you when you first arrived in Alaska?"

She slid across the seat and snuggled in close to him. "How could I forget?"

"And what did I say you needed?"

Victoria sighed. Contented, she rested her head on Buck's broad shoulder. "How well I remember your exact words. You said all I needed was a little northern exposure. And oh, how right you were!"

A Letter To Our Readers

Dear Reader:

In order that we might better contribute to your reading enjoyment, we would appreciate your taking a few minutes to respond to the following questions. We welcome your comments and read each form and letter we receive. When completed, please return to the following:

Rebecca Germany, Fiction Editor
Heartsong Presents
PO Box 719
Uhrichsville, Ohio 44683

1. Did you enjoy reading *Northern Exposure* by Joyce Livingston?

   ❑ Very much! I would like to see more books by this author!
   ❑ Moderately. I would have enjoyed it more if

   _____

   _____

2. Are you a member of **Heartsong Presents**? Yes ❑ No ❑
   If no, where did you purchase this book?_____

   _____

3. How would you rate, on a scale from 1 (poor) to 5 (superior), the cover design?_____

4. On a scale from 1 (poor) to 10 (superior), please rate the following elements.

   _____ Heroine   _____ Plot

   _____ Hero   _____ Inspirational theme

   _____ Setting   _____ Secondary characters

These characters were special because _____

_____

_____

6. How has this book inspired your life? _____

_____

_____

7. What settings would you like to see covered in future
   Heartsong Presents books? _____

_____

_____

8. What are some inspirational themes you would like to see
   treated in future books? _____

_____

_____

9. Would you be interested in reading other **Heartsong
   Presents** titles?   Yes ❑   No ❑

10. Please check your age range:
    ❑ Under 18   ❑ 18-24   ❑ 25-34
    ❑ 35-45   ❑ 46-55   ❑ Over 55

Name _____

Occupation _____

Address _____

City _____ State _____ Zip _____

Email _____

LOVE AFLOAT

Time, tides, and the hand of God draw the hearts of four couples together in these delightful tales. Authors Kim Comeaux, Linda Goodnight, JoAnn A. Grote, and Diann Hunt weave four engaging stories of romance on the water.

Ride the waves as God leads His children through adversity, and go with the flow as love floods the hearts of four young couples. This collection of inspiring romances will certainly be a treasure on your bookshelves.

paperback, 352 pages, 5 ³/₁₆" x 8"

❤ ❤ ❤ ❤ ❤ ❤ ❤ ❤ ❤ ❤ ❤ ❤ ❤ ❤ ❤ ❤ ❤

❤ ❤ ❤ ❤ ❤ ❤ ❤ ❤ ❤ ❤ ❤ ❤ ❤ ❤ ❤ ❤ ❤

·······Presents·······

Great Inspirational Romance at a Great Price!

Heartsong Presents books are inspirational romances in contemporary and historical settings, designed to give you an enjoyable, spirit-lifting reading experience. You can choose wonderfully written titles from some of today's best authors like Hannah Alexander, Irene B. Brand, Yvonne Lehman, Tracie Peterson, and many others.

When ordering quantities less than twelve, above titles are $2.95 each.
Not all titles may be available at time of order.

Hearts♥ng Presents
Love Stories Are Rated G!

That's for godly, gratifying, and of course, great! If you love a thrilling love story but don't appreciate the sordidness of some popular paperback romances, **Heartsong Presents** is for you. In fact, **Heartsong Presents** is the *only inspirational romance book club* featuring love stories where Christian faith is the primary ingredient in a marriage relationship.

Sign up today to receive your first set of four never before published Christian romances. Send no money now; you will receive a bill with the first shipment. You may cancel at any time without obligation, and if you aren't completely satisfied with any selection, you may return the books for an immediate refund!

Imagine. . .four new romances every four weeks—two historical, two contemporary—with men and women like you who long to meet the one God has chosen as the love of their lives. . . all for the low price of $9.97 postpaid.

To join, simply complete the coupon below and mail to the address provided. **Heartsong Presents** romances are rated G for another reason: They'll arrive *Godspeed!*